THE *Forever* COWBOY

A Shanahan Match
Calling on the Matchmaker
Saved by the Matchmaker
A Wager with the Matchmaker
Marrying the Matchmaker

Bride Ships: New Voyages
Finally His Bride
His Treasured Bride
His Perfect Bride
His Unforgettable Bride

Bride Ships Series
A Reluctant Bride
The Runaway Bride
A Bride of Convenience
Almost a Bride

Orphan Train Series
An Awakened Heart: A Novella
With You Always
Together Forever
Searching for You

Beacons of Hope Series
Out of the Storm: A Novella
Love Unexpected
Hearts Made Whole
Undaunted Hope
Forever Safe
Never Forget

Lost Princesses Series

Always: Prequel Novella

Evermore

Foremost

Hereafter

Noble Knights Series

The Vow: Prequel Novella

An Uncertain Choice

A Daring Sacrifice

For Love & Honor

A Loyal Heart

A Worthy Rebel

Waters of Time Series

Come Back to Me

Never Leave Me

Stay With Me

Wait for Me

THE *Forever* COWBOY

JODY HEDLUND

NORTHERN LIGHTS PRESS

The Forever Cowboy
Northern Lights Press
© 2025 by Jody Hedlund
Jody Hedlund Print Edition
ISBN 979-8-9896277-7-6

Jody Hedlund www.jodyhedlund.com

This is a work of historical reconstruction; the appearances of certain historical figures are accordingly inevitable. All other characters are products of the author's imagination. Any resemblance to actual events or locales or persons, living or dead, is entirely coincidental.

Cover Design by roseannawhitedesigns.com
Cover images from Shutterstock

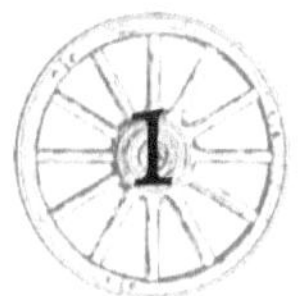

A thunderous pounding against the front door startled Violet Berkley awake. She bolted upright in bed, the comforter falling away and exposing her to the chill of the unheated upstairs bedroom on the cold November night.

Beside her, Hyacinth stirred. "What's wrong, Vi?"

"Father's in trouble again." Violet knew that even without any other information. His trouble had always been the reason for late-night callers.

The thudding on the door resounded again, this time accompanied by a voice. "Open up, Marvin, and pay me!"

The words echoed through the thin walls and windows of the house they'd rented from the bank when their family had moved to Breckenridge a year and a half ago.

Yes, a year and a half was about as long as they ever lasted in one place.

Violet hugged her arms around her body as if that could ward off the frustration—and helplessness. But of course, it didn't.

"I even gave you a few extra days," came the voice outside. "No more delays."

Footsteps squeaked in the hallway outside the bedroom, then began to descend the stairway. Hesitant, reluctant steps belonging to Father.

It was obvious he didn't want to answer the door, but what choice did he have if he didn't want to wake up the whole neighborhood? If that happened, everyone would know about their ruinous situation and the fact that Mr. Marvin Berkley was a gambler—and an abysmal one at that.

Maybe people would find out soon enough anyway, because this time Mother wasn't alive to come to Father's rescue. Even if she'd survived the influenza, her inheritance would have been of little help. The years had whittled it down to almost nothing. After Mother's death, Violet had used the last of it to pay the doctor's bills and the burial fees in Williamsburg. She'd only had enough left for the train tickets for her and Hyacinth to return to Colorado.

Violet slid her hand under the comforter and clasped Hyacinth's fingers, which were steady but cold. Hyacinth was only three years younger than Violet's twenty-two years and didn't need coddling, but Violet had promised on Mother's deathbed that she would look out for her sister.

Although as sisters they shared the same sable-black hair, pine-green eyes, thick dark lashes, and comely figures, that was where the similarities in appearance ended. Violet had more delicate, defined features compared to Hyacinth's natural, open beauty. Violet had pale skin that made her look like she rarely spent time in the sun, while Hyacinth's skin was a soft tan with freckles on her nose and forehead. Violet was shorter and smaller boned, and Hyacinth was slender and willowy.

Father finished descending the stairs, and his footsteps echoed in the front hallway. A moment later, the door squealed open on its hinges. From the sounds of the voices entering the house, there were at least two visitors.

"Can I get you something to drink?" Father asked as the door clicked closed.

"Pay up, Marvin." The same fellow spoke again.

"You've been good to me, Claude." Father's tone was placating. "You've shown me grace. No one else is quite as nice as you."

Violet shivered at the familiar compliments her father was so good at giving—compliments that meant nothing except for what he could gain through them.

Hyacinth squeezed Violet's hand as though to

reassure her that they would face this new trial together and she would take care of Violet in the same way that Violet was taking care of her. But how could they promise each other anything now that Mother's inheritance was gone and they had no way to provide for themselves anymore?

"I have been good to you." Claude didn't sound flattered by Father. "But I can only be good for so long."

"Of course, of course. But surely you can understand that I've run into issues."

"That's just an excuse, Marvin."

"My daughters used up the remainder of my wife's money, and now I have to look elsewhere for assistance."

A burst of indignation shot through Violet. Was Father blaming his financial woes upon her and Hyacinth? How dare he? They'd arrived home less than a week ago and had no part in the poor choices that had landed him in debt over the recent weeks and months.

"Your daughters?"

"Yes, I have two."

"Are they pretty?"

"The most beautiful girls in the world."

Hyacinth released a soft growl. "I hate when he says that."

Violet disliked it too. How often had she heard Father tell her, Hyacinth, and Mother that? Countless times.

She supposed on some level he meant it, because deep

down, Father was a good man, and he thought the world of them. But that didn't change the fact that he loved the thrill of the gaming table and always went back to it, no matter how many times he'd promised Mother he would stay away.

Another voice spoke, but too low for Violet to hear—probably one of Claude's companions relaying information to him.

"Tiny says he's seen them with you," Claude continued, "and that you're not exaggerating about their beauty."

Something in Claude's tone sent a prickle of unease up Violet's backbone.

"No," Father said. "Don't even think about it."

"Think about what?"

"You want to use my daughters to pay off my debt."

Hyacinth huffed a protest.

Violet quickly cupped her sister's mouth to keep her from saying anything and giving away their eavesdropping.

"Not in the way you're thinking, Marvin." Claude spoke smoothly. "I have enough soiled doves."

At the euphemism for *prostitute*, Violet was the one to release a gasp, and her spine turned as straight and rigid as a silver candlestick.

"Thank the good Lord." Father at least had the grace to sound distressed.

"No, I need more dancehall girls. The prettier, the better."

"Dancehall girls?" Father's question was loaded with indignation. "Of course not. My girls are decent and God-fearing and will make good matches."

The voices were low for a moment with the newcomers conversing. This Claude had to be a manager or owner of one of the many saloons that populated Breckenridge. Most had gaming tables, and her father had probably gambled at all of them.

"You should know"—Claude spoke again—"my prettiest and most popular dance girls can do forty to fifty dances in an evening and make more in one night than a fellow can make in a month of mining."

Violet had heard of dancehall girls who let the men pay to take turns dancing with them. She'd once seen several such women when she'd been with her mother outside a saloon in Denver, waiting for Father to come out. Even if dancehall women were considered "ladies" by most men, they dressed scandalously, plastered their cheeks with rouge, and had no self-respect.

Her father fell silent.

He wasn't considering Claude's offer, was he?

Violet shook her head. No, he wouldn't. In spite of his faults, he still loved them. Didn't he?

Hyacinth broke free from Violet's grasp on her mouth and sat up. "He'd better not," she whispered hotly.

"He won't," Violet whispered back.

"I don't let the fellows disrespect my dance girls." Claude's voice dropped so that Violet almost couldn't hear him. "No inappropriate comments or touching."

Violet shuddered. Regardless of Claude's rules, what kind of woman would ever consider such a position? Only someone in a truly distressing situation.

"With both of your girls working for me," Claude said, "you might be able to pay off your debt in three months."

"Three months?" Father's question held a note of surprise.

"Maybe four."

Violet didn't move. Hyacinth seemed to have stopped breathing. Was her sister waiting, like she was, for their father to declare that the proposal was ridiculous and he would never subject his daughters to that kind of work, especially because he was responsible for his problems?

But why would Father take responsibility for his debts now after years of having Mother fix his financial woes?

"Listen, Marvin." Claude's voice cut through the stillness of the night. "I heard you got fired from the bank."

Fired? Violet's heartbeat came to an abrupt halt. Father had told them he'd taken a leave from the bank to grieve for Mother. He hadn't mentioned anything about losing his job. Was that why he'd telegrammed for them to return? He'd said he missed them, wanted to be a family again, and promised to take care of them. But what if he'd hoped enough of Mother's inheritance remained to get him out of his newest trouble?

Violet's shoulders sank, and she lowered her head. She already knew the answer to her own question. Father was a liar. He always had been and always would be.

"Give me your daughters to work in the dancehall," Claude said, "and I'll let you rent a room from me and dock it from their pay."

Of course, without Father's job at the bank, they would no longer be eligible to live in their house. They would have to move. But with Father unemployed and penniless, where would they go? And how would they survive?

They would figure out something.

Violet expelled a tight breath. She wasn't as strong as Mother, and she wasn't as resourceful. However, she would assure Father that they could get through this together, that somehow they would find a way to survive.

"I don't know, Claude." Father's voice was laced with defeat. "Can I have some time to think about the offer?"

Don't know? Think about the offer? What in heaven's name was Father saying?

Anger began to burn along Violet's nerves. There was no thinking about it. She and Hyacinth would never ever resort to becoming dancehall girls, not for any reason—

not to survive and most certainly not to help their father repay his debts.

There was more low conversation, likely between Claude and his companion—Tiny.

"You've had all the time you're going to get." This time Claude's tone was hard. "Either pay me the money tonight, or give me your word that your daughters will work for me."

"But, Claude—"

"Your money or your daughters."

Father didn't respond.

Violet swallowed hard past a sudden lump in her throat. Father loved them. He wouldn't hand them over to Claude.

Hyacinth sat up now too, her body stiff.

The silence stretched.

"Well?" Claude asked irritably.

"You'll treat them respectfully?" Their father's voice held resignation.

The anger inside Violet fanned hotter. Was he really giving in to Claude's demand? What kind of Father would do such a thing? Even if he was desperate.

"Bring them over tomorrow," said Claude as the front door squealed open.

"I'll try."

"If you don't bring them, I'll send Tiny to fetch them."

A second later, the front door closed, and the house fell silent.

"Violet?" Hyacinth huffed out a breath loaded with frustration. "What should we do?"

"We're not working as dancing girls. That's for sure."

"I would rather die."

"Me too."

At their father's footsteps plodding up the staircase, Violet flopped back and tugged Hyacinth down beside her. Would he come and check on them? If he knew they were awake, maybe he'd try to talk to them tonight about his deal with Claude.

"Pretend to be asleep," Violet whispered as she yanked the covers back over them. Then she situated herself so that her back was facing the door, and Hyacinth did too.

A few moments later, Father's footsteps creaked in the hallway and then stopped outside their room. He paused and knocked.

Violet stiffened and could feel Hyacinth do the same.

The door clicked open, revealing a stream of light from his lantern.

Violet tried to breathe evenly and act like she was asleep.

Father was quiet, probably watching them. Then he sighed and closed the door.

Hyacinth began to move, but Violet stopped her with

a touch to her back. They lay motionless until Father's bedroom door closed and the springs of his bed groaned under his weight. Even then they waited.

All the while, the anger flamed inside Violet. They never should have listened to Father's plea to return to Colorado. They should have stayed in Williamsburg, Virginia, and used the last of the money to rent their room in the boarding house another month or two. Surely they could have found domestic work or teaching jobs in addition to the seamstress work they'd been taking in. That's what Mother, on her deathbed, had instructed Violet to do.

Now, with winter closing in, they were stuck in the high country of Colorado. The passes had already been difficult to traverse when they'd come by coach from Denver last week. With the past week of additional snow in the higher elevations, the traveling would be even more treacherous, if not impossible.

They might be stuck in the high country, but Violet refused to be stuck with Father and his horrible arrangement with Claude. If Claude sent his men, she and Hyacinth would refuse to go with them. No one could force them to become dancehall girls, could they?

As much as Violet wished she could resist her father and any other man who pressured her to do something, she knew she was as weak as her mother in that regard. Mother had always let Father talk her into doing what he wanted, and Violet couldn't chance staying and letting Father do the same to her.

The best course of action was for her and Hyacinth to leave home. They had to get away from his influence and his persuasive ways, at least until he came up with another plan to pay off his debts—one that didn't involve them.

But where could she and Hyacinth go?

Their mother had always been reticent and had kept to herself—probably because she'd been embarrassed by Father's gambling. As a result, they'd rarely mingled with people anywhere they'd lived.

It wasn't until they moved to Breckenridge that Violet had started to make more of an effort to socialize, mainly because she'd been longing to meet a man and begin a life and family of her own. Although she'd never been good at making friends, she'd forced herself to go out to local events. That's when she'd met Sterling Noble.

Oh, Sterling.

Her insides ached any time she allowed herself to think about him and their failed wedding, when she'd ruined things. There had been many times during the summer when she'd missed him and wondered what her life would have been like if she'd followed through with marrying him.

Unwanted images from that day months ago, in April, threatened to race through her mind, but she quickly forced the thoughts into the dark corners where they belonged. She had to focus on the current predicament.

The problem was that no one in Breckenridge or the rest of Summit County liked her. In fact, they resented her just as much now as they had before she'd left Colorado. That had become clear from the looks she'd received during her first day back in town.

The truth was, she had no one to turn to. She had no money to go anywhere. And she had no idea how to protect Hyacinth the way she'd promised Mother she would.

Was there anyone, anyone at all, who would be willing to help her? Anyone who cared about her even just a little?

A memory pushed to the surface—a memory of Sterling the night he'd proposed marriage at the miner's cabin. His caramel-brown eyes had peered up at her in the candlelight. They'd shone with a love so tender she'd quaked at the intensity. Yes, she'd been scared that night and had turned down his proposal. But his love had been so unforgettable and real and deep that she'd accepted his proposal a week later.

Surely he hadn't lost all his love for her over these past months. Maybe he wasn't so horribly angry with her for kissing another man on their wedding day and jilting him. Would he help her if she went to him and explained her situation?

No, she couldn't. Not if she had a shred of dignity

left. After running away from him and the love he'd offered, she couldn't grovel at his feet and beg him for help, could she?

Everything inside her protested going to him. What if he refused to see her? What if he told her to go away? It would be so humiliating. Then again, she'd humiliated him on their wedding day, so maybe she deserved the same in response.

Besides, Hyacinth despised Sterling—claimed he should have done more, and blamed him in part for the failed relationship. Hyacinth would definitely not want to have Sterling's help.

Violet buried her face in her pillow and wanted to cry out her frustration along with the resentment toward Father that she could no longer ignore. He should be protecting and providing for them. But had he ever?

"We have to go tonight, Violet," Hyacinth whispered. "Now, while Father is asleep."

Violet pushed up and listened. Father's faint snores rattled from the room across the hallway.

Hyacinth was right. Even though the night was dark and cold, they had to make their escape while they still could. But where could they go that Father—and Claude—wouldn't be able to find them?

Her mind raced again, trying to come up with more solutions. But there was only one. Even though it was a terrible option, she didn't know what else to do.

Another dead steer.

Sterling Noble pressed a hand against the steer's now motionless ribcage. Warmth lingered in the hide, but the breath of life was gone.

Kneeling in the hay mound next to Sterling, Beckett sat back on his heels, obviously realizing the same thing. They'd lost one more.

At least the creature wasn't suffering any longer. That was the only good thing about its death.

"Well, shoot." Beckett's voice dripped with his Southern drawl as he reached for the nearest railing of the stall and hoisted himself to his feet. Lanky but muscular, the ranch foreman had a layer of dark scruff on his face that made him look slightly dangerous. "At this rate, we'll lose half the herd before winter starts."

"No. We can't lose any more." Sterling lifted his cowboy hat and combed back the straggling strands that were in need of a trim. He'd been too busy with dying cattle to think about anything else, including haircuts.

It was only mid-November, and the worst of the cold and snow was yet to arrive at the Noble Ranch in the high mountain country of Colorado. That meant it was much too early for disease to be plaguing the herd.

But it was. The dreaded blackleg had shown up over the past week. It affected mostly the young cattle—the healthiest, between six months and two years—which would develop a sudden lameness, soon followed by muscle swelling. Most died within one or two days.

So far, nothing they'd done had stopped it from spreading—not even isolating the afflicted steers—and they'd lost close to twenty. To make matters worse, his newest breed, the Durfords—a mix of Herefords with Durham bulls—had been hit the hardest. More winter-hardy and providing a better cut of meat, the Durfords were the biggest source of income for the ranch.

Sterling blew out a tight breath as he took in the dozen or so other lame steers they'd brought into the barn. Several more were already down on their sides, in too much pain to stand, their bodies bloated. The others were resting in nearby stalls that usually held the cows and some of the youngest calves, which had all been moved to the horse barn to keep them safe.

Beckett cocked his head toward the door. "You go on and get some shut-eye—"

"I'm fine—"

"You've stayed the past three nights. Let me do it tonight." Beckett's eyes held a gravity that likely matched Sterling's. The ranch foreman was only a few years older than Sterling's twenty-six years and was like a brother. In fact, at times Beckett seemed more like family than his three flesh-and-blood brothers.

It didn't help that Mom and Dad, all three brothers, and both sisters were gone, leaving Sterling alone for the winter. Not that he minded running the ranch. He'd been doing that for the past three years anyway while Dad had shifted his focus to his silver mines in the hills to the west of Breckenridge.

Ranching was in Sterling's blood. He loved it more than he'd ever thought possible after his family had moved from Wisconsin to Colorado when he was only thirteen. Over the years, they'd worked hard as a family to build the biggest ranch in Summit County and one of the largest in all of Colorado.

Yes, he loved their ranch. But he'd never expected to be the only one here, the only one handling the responsibility and problems. Of course, he did have six full-time ranch hands living in the bunkhouse in addition to Beckett. There was also Alonzo, who did the cooking and errands and took care of the rest of the livestock— including the horses, goats, chickens, and half a dozen pigs.

So technically, Sterling wasn't alone. But the pressure to figure out how to save the cattle and keep the ranch successful was on his shoulders and no one else's.

"You need a break." Sticking a piece of hay in his mouth, Beckett tucked his fingers into his suspenders. "If any of the beeves worsen, I'll come get you."

Unable to hold back a yawn, Sterling scrubbed a hand over the stubble on his jaw and chin. If he hoped to be any good to the ranch and the sick cattle, he couldn't get sick himself. That meant he had to catch a few hours of sleep.

He climbed to his feet and stretched his back. At six feet three inches, he was the tallest of his brothers and had the largest frame with the most muscle. All of them had their dad's brown hair and brown eyes. But Sterling was the most rugged with his weathered, bronzed skin and tough, work-honed body.

"All right." Sterling shuffled through the haymow. "Send one of the fellows for the veterinarian at first light."

Thatcher Hoyt had already been out to the ranch earlier in the week and had officially diagnosed the disease and let them know that blackleg was becoming a huge problem on ranches throughout the West. He'd spouted some technical causes for the disease, what he'd called a bacterium that lived in the soil and manure.

Thatcher had a Latin name for the bacterium that Sterling couldn't remember and claimed that the tiny critters were so small that no one could see them, not even the cattle. But somehow, apparently, the cattle could ingest them. Once inside their stomachs and intestines, the bacterium got into the blood and then into the muscles.

The veterinarian had said most of the time the disease was fatal, and the best thing to do was to try to isolate the sick. Thatcher had also offered to vaccinate the steers in an effort to stave off the disease. But he'd warned that the vaccination methods were unproven and had met with varying success. Some had even been more lethal than the disease.

Sterling hadn't wanted to vaccinate and chance having the whole herd die, so over the past few days, they'd cleaned and scoured the barns, the holding pens, and the nearby fields, getting rid of the waste and putting out clean hay.

But the cattle were still getting sick. At the rate they were dying, he would lose the whole herd within a few weeks. He had to try something else.

"Let's get Thatcher back over here and talk more about the vaccination."

Beckett gave a curt nod. "Will do, boss."

Grabbing his coat off the end of a pitchfork, where he'd tossed it, Sterling opened the barn door to the blackness of the night, broken by the light of the half-moon in the cloudless sky. It was well past midnight, probably already one or two in the morning.

The barn wasn't heated, but the natural warmth from the livestock kept it from getting too cold. The well-constructed walls blocked the wind.

Without the protection, frosty air hit his face, bringing with it the scent of damp soil after the snow they'd had a few days ago. A gust whipped at him, the frigid bite stinging his face and arms.

He shrugged into his coat, then picked up his pace as he crossed the ranch yard. His boots crunched against the frozen ground, the only sound except for the occasional snort from the cattle penned into the pasture closest to the barns. The night noises from insects and other small critters were gone, since most animals had migrated to lower elevations for the winter or were hibernating.

The house windows were all dark, not a single lantern lit to help guide the way—not that he needed the light. He was familiar enough with the ranch to get around blindfolded if need be. Even so, his chest squeezed with the loneliness that had been bothering him lately. Maybe that was another reason he wasn't keen on everyone abandoning the ranch for the winter. Because the loneliness had a way of creeping up on him whenever he was in the house.

Even their faithful maid Jo-Jo was gone. She'd accompanied Mom, Dad, and Scarlet for their trip to Coleman's college graduation. At twenty-five, Coleman was finishing law school and following in Dad's footsteps, the dutiful son who had done everything Dad had wanted by going to college and getting an education.

Sterling knew he'd been a disappointment to Dad by refusing to go. His dad had argued with him that he would have more opportunities with a specialty and by bettering himself. He'd wanted more for Sterling than just the ranch. But Sterling had insisted the ranch was all he'd ever need, and he'd vowed to his dad that he could make the ranch successful without an education.

He stifled a sigh. Right now, with the number of cattle dying, he was failing to live up to his vow. He didn't want Dad to arrive home and find the ranch worse than ever. No, he wanted his dad to return home to a thriving and even bigger ranch.

Ultimately, Sterling needed to prove he hadn't made a mistake in staying at the ranch instead of going to college the way Dad had wanted. More than anything, he didn't want his dad to look at him with disappointment and say *I told you so.*

Thankfully, Sterling still had time to turn things around. While his family was in the East, they planned to also visit Paxton at his college and meet up with some of Dad's friends from his law-school days. After that, they were heading by train to stay with relatives in Wisconsin, where they would spend the holidays and the rest of the winter before returning to Colorado in the spring.

At least Hazel was living on High C Ranch only two miles away. Sterling saw her once in a while, mainly at church on Sundays. She was happily married to Maverick Oakley, his best friend, and she was still the broodmare manager and planned to keep working until she had her baby in the spring.

Sterling slowed his steps as the outline of the large home took shape, with its Victorian-style flourishes and design. Painted white and trimmed in black, the beautiful house had been built a few years after they'd started bringing in a profit from their ranch. With five bedrooms upstairs, it had been more than adequate for their large family.

His gaze snagged on the front window of the formal parlor, the largest room—the room where he'd planned to marry Violet.

"No," he whispered harshly. "No thoughts of her."

For months after she'd run off, he hadn't been able to keep himself from dwelling on how much he despised her for what she'd done. Doing so had only made him all the angrier so that he'd thought about her more.

Finally he'd decided he had to cut all ties to her, even the negative ones, and pretend she'd never existed. To do so, he'd worked himself until he was so tired he couldn't think about anything. Eventually, he'd dwelt on her less and less until she'd faded to the background. He'd been doing well over the last several months, keeping his mind from veering into unwanted territory.

Until last week…when at church, Hazel had let it slip that Violet and Hyacinth had returned from the East. Apparently their mother had died, and they'd come back to live with their father.

The moment Sterling had heard the news, he'd felt a momentary pang of sorrow for Violet, knowing how close she'd been to her mother. Of course, he hadn't wanted to feel anything for Violet—not even sympathy—but it had been there anyway.

Ever since Sunday, thoughts of her had been coming with more frequency. Maybe that was the reason why he'd been staying up every night with the sick cattle—to have a diversion, something to hold his attention, anything to keep him busy.

Now the minute he was done working, his mind went right to her.

He halted on the flagstone path that led to the porch spread across the front of the house. He wouldn't allow himself to think about Violet for the rest of the short night. He'd already given enough to that woman, and he didn't owe her another thought, not even the tiniest one. That's why he was considering skipping church this week, so that he didn't run into her there. He didn't want to see her again and would have been happy if she'd never returned to Summit County.

He blew out an exasperated breath.

Should he consider the possibility of finding another woman? His sister Scarlet had told him multiple times over the past summer that he should move on to someone else.

The problem was, he hadn't been ready for another relationship during the summer. Maybe he'd still been reeling from Violet's running away from the wedding. Maybe he'd been scared of being rejected again. Maybe he'd been hoping time would heal him.

Whatever the case, it was obviously time to force himself to be ready—to go to social gatherings and to mingle with women again.

Or maybe he should send away for a mail-order bride the same way Beckett had. The bride was planning on coming in the spring, and Beckett intended to have built a small home for her by then—a home on the ranch so that he could continue to be the foreman, a home close to where Sterling had planned to build his.

The veterinarian had also put an ad into one of the matrimonial catalogs and had been expecting his bride to arrive all autumn. Unfortunately, she hadn't shown up yet.

With the way men outnumbered the women in the high country, the marriageable young women were snapped up so quickly it was difficult for even stellar men like Beckett and Thatcher to have a chance at finding a wife.

Sterling shook his head at going the mail-order bride route. He wasn't that desperate. Not yet.

The question was—would he ever be able to love another woman?

He peered up at the stars blinking in the universe. He'd thought Violet was the only one for him, the glowing sun swinging into his orbit, the brilliant light to his life. But it turned out she'd only been a shooting star, there one moment and gone the next.

Anger sliced through him again—anger at her, at himself, at God, at everything and everyone.

He gave a curt shake of his head. He didn't want to feel that anger again, which meant he had to keep from dwelling on her and all that had happened.

He started down the path again, his footsteps slapping against the stones. He just needed to go to bed. He was so tired that the moment his head hit his pillow, he'd fall into oblivion and put her out of his head.

As he started up the steps, movement and a soft voice from one side of the porch brought him to a standstill.

Someone was there.

He quickly pushed aside his coat and gripped the handle of his revolver. He narrowed his gaze on the far area, withdrew his gun, and pointed it at the outline of a person who was rising from one of the rocking chairs.

"Who's there?" He had no idea who would be out at this time of the night, especially when it was so cold.

"Hi, Sterling," came a shaking voice, a familiar voice, one he'd never wanted to hear again.

The very sound of it sent his heartbeat into an out-of-control gallop. His whole body stiffened, and his mouth went suddenly dry.

She took a step forward. "It's me, Violet."

He didn't need her to say her name. He would recognize her voice in a crowd of a thousand women.

"What are you doing here?" His question came out harsh and filled with all the bitterness he'd been holding inside since she'd looked at him on their wedding day after kissing another man and said: *I can't marry you! Not when I don't know if I even love you.*

"I need help, Sterling." Again, her voice wobbled. From fear? Or from the cold? Or both?

He hesitated, but then he holstered his gun and finished climbing the stairs. Why was he giving her even a moment of his time? His consideration. "Go home. You're not welcome here."

Without another glance, he steeled his shoulders and started toward the door.

"I knew we shouldn't have come here," another voice whispered, this one different but decidedly feminine. "He's such an arrogant oaf."

He halted only a few steps from the door. Had Violet brought Hyacinth with her? If so, had they walked from town?

"Hush," Violet said softly.

From the corner of his eyes, he could see Violet straighten and face him squarely. "Please, Sterling." Her voice was definitely shaking, or perhaps she was shaking, no doubt from the frigid night. How long had they been waiting on the porch? It wouldn't take long for her to be frozen to the bone—not with how thin she was.

He silently cursed. Violet wasn't his problem, and he couldn't worry about her.

"We need a place to hide," she continued. "Maybe for a couple of days, just until—"

"Not here. Find someplace else." He took two more steps to reach the door.

"I don't know where else to go."

He opened the door and swung it wide. "Go home."

"We can't." Her tone held a note of desperation, and she started crossing the porch toward him.

He stepped inside, needing to slam the front door behind him and block her out of his sight. He didn't want to look at her perfect body, didn't want to see her beautiful face, and didn't want to peer into her stunning eyes. Because if he did, he wasn't sure he'd be able to walk away from her tonight. One tiny glimpse of her had always rendered him useless and weak and powerless against her charm. He had the feeling that hadn't changed, even though he'd tried so hard to free himself from her power.

He grabbed the door and started to close it against an invisible hand that seemed to be forcing it open.

She stopped only a foot away from him. "My dad made a bargain with a guy named Claude to have Hyacinth and me become dancehall girls."

"What?" He released the door and pivoted to face her. He hadn't heard her correctly, had he?

Violet was close enough that he could reach out and touch her if he wanted to—which he didn't. The moon cast a glow over her face, revealing the long lines of her jaw and cheeks, the perfectly slender nose, and the smoothness of her skin. Beneath the hood of her coat, her dark hair was pulled back in a long braid, but wisps framed her face.

Keen longing shot through him. Holy sweet heaven. He'd missed seeing her. Missed her presence. Missed her voice. Missed her beauty. Missed everything about her.

"My father owes Claude a great deal of money," she continued, "and so Claude said we could work for him as dance girls to pay off his debt."

Dance girls?

Sterling could only blink at the allegation.

Mr. Berkley was a bank teller, which was a good and decent job. He was an upright, law-abiding, and well-respected citizen. There had never been any issues before. Why would Violet accuse her father of something so terrible now?

Her high brows slanted above her wide eyes that were framed by lush, dark lashes. He couldn't clearly distinguish the green color of her eyes, but he could see the distress in every line of her expression.

She wouldn't be able to act so upset if she wasn't telling the truth, would she?

On the other hand, she'd been a good actor with him, making him believe she loved him when she never really had.

He crossed his arms over his chest and lifted his chin. "I don't believe you."

She hugged her coat closer to her body, rubbing her mittened hands up and down her arms, likely for warmth. In the same motion, she shuddered. "If my father doesn't turn us over, Claude said he'll send his men to come get us."

Sterling tried to glare.

Her eyes turned glassy with unshed tears.

No, he wouldn't let her tears move him. Not anymore, never again. He had to walk away.

Before he could move, her chin quivered, then her teeth began to chatter, even though she seemed to be trying to clamp her lips together.

She was freezing.

He peered through the dark to the edge of the porch, where Hyacinth was huddling in the other rocking chair. No doubt she was freezing too.

The battle raging inside him escalated—a battle he was already losing and perhaps had lost from the moment he'd realized she was on the porch. As much as he wanted to stay away from her and keep up the rampart he'd built to protect himself, he couldn't walk away from two people who were in need of warmth and shelter. Not when the alternative would mean leaving them outside to face the frigid November temperatures.

He didn't know what the truth was about her situation with her father. He had the feeling she was holding something back, that there was more to the story than she was sharing. Even though he absolutely didn't want to invite her into his home, he would never turn his back on someone in need, not even his worst enemy.

Was that why she was here? Because she knew that? Or had she come to torment him?

Whatever the case, he had to get both women out of the cold.

Expelling a sigh, he stood back from the door and waved her inside. "You and Hyacinth can come in and warm up. Then you'll need to be on your way."

She dropped her head, but not before he heard a soft sob. She nodded, seemed to be getting herself under control, and then spoke quietly. "I know I don't deserve your help, but thank you for giving it to me anyway."

Hyacinth was already rising and stumbling toward Violet. The younger woman was shaking worse than Violet.

He was doing the right thing by inviting them in. Wasn't he?

Right or wrong, Violet Berkley was walking back into his life. He would just have to make sure she walked back out tonight as soon as possible.

The warmth of a stove had never felt so good before.

Violet rubbed her frozen fingers together and wiggled her stiff toes. Standing beside her in the Nobles' kitchen, in front of the blazing fire of the open stove, Hyacinth was doing the same thing.

They'd discarded their mittens and hoods but hadn't shed their coats. Violet doubted Sterling would let them stay long anyway. From the rigid way he stood near the worktable, he was clearly waiting to evict them as soon as they were warm.

Their valises still sat outside on the porch, filled with as much of their clothing and belongings as they could carry. They'd dressed in warm layers and multiple stockings before creeping out of the house and had made their way out of town via the back alleys. Once on the road north, they'd remained in the shadows.

Hyacinth had protested when she'd finally realized

where Violet was taking them, but by that point, they'd come too far to turn back. Thankfully, they hadn't met anyone during the four-mile trek to the Noble home. They'd walked briskly in an effort to stay warm, but by the time they'd reached the ranch gate, they'd both begun to shiver.

When they'd knocked on the door without receiving an answer, Violet had decided the best option was to wait a short while before trying again. Since Sterling was an early riser, she'd guessed he would be rousing soon enough.

The longer they'd waited in the cold, and the stiffer her limbs had grown, the more she'd contemplated breaking into one of the barns in an attempt to find some warmth. She'd been about to suggest that option when Sterling had stepped out of the cattle barn.

She hadn't been able to view him well in the darkness, but she'd seen enough of his tall, muscular frame to know it was him. Not only that, but he had a distinctive swagger to his step—a swagger that held the same confidence and determination she'd first noticed about him last year when she'd been new in Breckenridge.

Lowering her lashes now, she glanced sideways at him. He filled the kitchen with his overpowering presence the same way he'd always filled every room. Tonight, with his dark coat hanging to his knees and his hat pulled low, he looked forbidding.

His maple-sugar-brown hair was longer than it had been earlier in the year and curled against his coat collar. The dark scruff on his face was thicker. And his features were more rugged and weathered. Somehow he was more handsome tonight than when she'd first met him, although she wasn't sure how that was possible since he'd had killer looks all along, making her weak every time she was around him.

He'd stuffed his hands into his pockets, and his shoulders were slumped, as though exhaustion was weighing him down.

"I'm sorry we're keeping you from bed," she offered. There had to be a reason—probably not a good one—for why he was up so late. There also had to be a reason why his family hadn't heard her knocking and didn't appear to be home. As much as she wanted to inquire about how he and his family were doing, she kept her questions to herself. She'd lost the right to ask when she'd broken things off with him.

"Can you go stay in a hotel in town?" His question was abrupt and to the point.

Hyacinth huffed. "I told you we shouldn't have come here, that he'd be too full of himself to help." She tossed Sterling a dark glare.

Violet stifled a sigh. She had nothing left beyond a few pennies, but she was too embarrassed to admit that to Sterling. Instead, she shrugged and focused on the flames dancing. "I thought we'd be safer if we were away from town."

"Who is Claude?" Again his tone contained no warmth.

"I don't know."

"Why does your father owe him money?"

She hesitated. The whole truth was much too embarrassing. Sterling already hated her, and he would think even less of her after learning about her father's problems. When they'd been courting, her mother had done everything she could to hide all evidence of Father's problems, probably hoping Sterling wouldn't realize how broken their family really was.

How could Violet admit it now?

"Tell me the truth." Sterling's tone was cold and impersonal.

"It shouldn't matter," Hyacinth murmured to Violet, but loud enough for Sterling to hear. "He should be willing to help regardless of everything, and he's not."

As Violet shifted from the stove to face him, she felt as though in some ways she was looking at a stranger. Gone was the loving and kind man who had adored her in every capacity, who had revered her like she was a princess, who had granted her every wish, and who had loved her like no one else ever had.

He had been too good to be true, and the way he'd treated her had been too good as well. She'd known it would only be a matter of time before he realized she wasn't a princess worthy of his adoration.

Now he knew. And now he was treating her like a normal person. Well, maybe he was treating her like she had a plague that she would pass on just by breathing near him. But what did she expect?

At least he'd let them inside to warm up. She'd bought herself some time to figure out what to do next. Could she go and stay with Hazel and Maverick? Sterling's sister had become a friend of sorts, but not anyone close. From the little gossip Violet had heard so far during her time back in Breckenridge, she knew Hazel was expecting a baby. Could they really impose on her?

She'd considered Reverend Livingston and his wife. But they lived in town and had a small child. Violet didn't want to put them in the middle of her issues with her father.

"Why is your father having financial problems?" Sterling's question cut through the silence of the kitchen.

Since he was persisting in his interrogation, she had no way to get around telling him the truth, as mortifying as it was. She swallowed all the resistance that crowded in her throat. "Because of the gaming tables."

"He gambles?"

"Yes." She stared at the wooden floor, unable to meet Sterling's gaze and the censure sure to be there. Respectable men did not go to saloons and gamble away their earnings, especially when they had families to support.

Sterling was quiet.

Hyacinth sighed with exasperation, but then slipped her hand into Violet's, supporting her as always.

Violet grasped her sister's hand, needing the encouragement more now than ever. If she'd thought life had been challenging before, those problems couldn't compare to the trouble she was facing tonight.

"I don't believe you," Sterling finally said, his voice testy.

Her gaze snapped up to his. This was the second time he'd said those exact words. Why was he doubting everything she was telling him? "We may not have worked out, Sterling, but I was always honest—"

"Honest?" His brows rose, revealing darkly bitter eyes.

She took a rapid step back and almost bumped into the stove.

"You lied about our relationship all along, pretending to love me when you didn't."

"That's not true!" Was it partially true? Had she pretended to love Sterling?

Were they really having this conversation here and now? She supposed it was long overdue. But tonight, when she was in the middle of a crisis, didn't seem like the right time to fight with him over why their relationship hadn't worked.

"You never loved me." His glare dared her to defy him.

Love was a strong word, and she wasn't sure if what she'd felt for Sterling actually had been love. But that didn't diminish the feelings she'd harbored for him. "Of course I cared about you. Why else would I agree to marry you?"

"You didn't care about anyone but yourself."

Hyacinth released a mocking laugh. "That's absolutely perfect coming from you."

Violet yanked on her sister's arm. She didn't need her sister making matters worse. "Stay out of this. Please."

Hyacinth rolled her eyes but clamped her lips together.

Violet returned her attention to Sterling, to his shadowed face and hurt-filled eyes.

Was he right? Maybe she had only been thinking of herself. She'd been scared when he'd proposed. She'd told herself the fear was normal for a bride, that the uncertainties would go away, that the doubts would diminish.

But as the wedding had drawn closer, the fear had begun to strangle her and wake her up at night. She'd spent less and less time with Sterling, and he'd been so busy with the calving that he hadn't noticed.

When the day of the wedding had finally arrived, she'd been sleep-deprived and jittery and hadn't been thinking straight. Because if she'd used an ounce of reason, she would have met with Sterling privately and talked with him about her fears and asked him if they could postpone the wedding.

Instead, she'd gone to his house and gotten ready for the ceremony in his sisters' room. By that point, the guests had all started arriving—so many people. When she'd told Hyacinth and Mother she needed a few moments by herself, they'd left the room. She'd used the opportunity to slip down a servant's staircase and out the back door. She'd needed to think, to catch her breath, to draw in the strength to persevere with the union—a union her parents, especially her mother, had been so happy about.

Once outside, all Violet had wanted to do was run home, crawl into bed, and pull the covers over her head. When Maverick had come around the house and spotted her, she hadn't known what to do. All the questions she'd been asking herself had surfaced. Maybe Sterling truly did love her. But was his love strong enough? Would he always love her more than everything else? Or would his interests and hobbies one day mean more to him than she did? What would happen when she was no longer first in his life?

The questions had been swirling through her head, and when Maverick had picked her up to carry her back inside, she hadn't known how to stop him other than to kiss him. It had been a horrible thing to do. But in her confusion—and maybe even in her unconscious effort to sabotage the wedding—she'd wondered if what she felt for Sterling could happen with Maverick. She'd reasoned that Sterling wasn't so special and that she'd allowed herself to fall for the first man who'd shown interest in her.

The kiss with Maverick had been perfunctory and bland, like kissing a lumpy gourd. The experience had been nothing at all like Sterling's kisses. Even so, when Sterling had come rushing out of the house after witnessing the kiss with Maverick, she'd pushed him away.

She couldn't remember everything she'd told him, but the moment had been painful and tense. She'd run away from him to the barn, where her mother and sister had found her sobbing in a horse stall. Mother had arranged for the carriage she'd rented to come around to the barn and pick them up and take them back to Breckenridge.

Sterling had tried to talk to her, had come to their house, had begged her not to push him away. In spite of his pleas, she'd refused to talk to him or see him before she left town for Williamsburg with Mother and Hyacinth. Even though Sterling had written to her a few times, she hadn't been able to make herself respond.

There was no doubt about it. Sterling's accusation that she hadn't cared about anyone but herself was true.

She'd been selfish and had only considered her fears and insecurities.

His dark gaze held no love, no kindness, no pleading now. No, it contained contempt.

"You're right." The confession fell out easily. "I only thought about myself. I was horribly selfish."

Hyacinth shook her head, but thankfully didn't say more.

He didn't respond, pressing his lips together with obvious displeasure.

Violet knew the breakup had caused him pain, and she'd wanted to apologize many times over the past months. But she hadn't known how to start. This wasn't exactly the best moment for the long-overdue apology, yet she had to say something. "I regret the way I handled everything. I should have done so many things differently."

His gaze was riveted to hers, waiting for more.

"I'm sorry for not being more honest with you earlier in our relationship."

His jaw twitched.

Was he expecting her to apologize for leaving him? For giving him up? For not going through with marrying him?

Was she sorry for that? Maybe a part of her was. At the very least, she wanted him to understand that she was sorry for how she'd gone about it all.

"I wish I hadn't been so afraid," she said hesitantly. "I should have talked with you privately about my feelings, so that you knew it wasn't you and that the breakup was because of me."

"I get it." The bitterness was back in his voice. "You're apologizing after all this time, tonight…so that I'll help you."

"No." Dismay coursed through her. "That didn't cross my mind. I was apologizing because you brought up my shortfall of being selfish, and I was agreeing with you."

"Since you understand my perspective so well, then maybe you'll understand why I don't want you here." His expression was lined with a stubbornness she had forgotten about. Sterling Noble was an obstinate man when he wanted to be.

"Since you clearly want to get rid of me so badly, then fine, I'll go." Hyacinth had been right. It had been a mistake to come here.

Sterling didn't step aside and wave toward the door as she expected. Instead, he seemed to be waiting for her to make the first move.

She needed to buy them more time to come up with a viable plan. "Would you let us stay in the kitchen near the stove until dawn?"

His attention shifted to the clock on the wall, next to the cabinet containing all of the cooking supplies. The timepiece read three o'clock. That meant dawn was still a few hours away. Would that be enough time to figure out another plan?

Sterling still didn't budge.

"Just a few more hours, and then you won't ever have to see me again."

Finally he nodded curtly. "I'm going to bed. I don't want to find you here when I get up." With that, he turned and stalked out of the kitchen. His footsteps thudded through the hallway and then up the stairs. A moment later, his bedroom door closed.

Only then did Violet allow herself to take a full breath.

"That went well," Hyacinth said sarcastically.

Violet began to pace, too flustered to sit.

She'd thought Sterling would have had more decency, that he would have been kinder and more forgiving. He was not the man she'd thought he was.

Or she'd hurt him more than she'd realized and he was still hurting.

Hyacinth held her hands out toward the stove again. "Guess we're back where we started, with no place to go."

"Don't worry. I'll think of something." Violet paced to the tin sink built into the wall, to the worktable, then to the hutch.

Sterling had always been open and genuine with his feelings—maybe too much too soon for her. But he'd been real. The vision of Sterling on his knees in front of her that night at the miner's cabin in Devil's Glen came back to her again.

The miner's cabin…

She halted in front of the hutch even as her pulse jolted forward. The rustic log cabin, once used by miners in the early days of Colorado's gold rush, belonged to the Nobles and was set on a piece of land they'd purchased in the foothills to the west of the ranch. The Nobles' ranch hands sometimes stayed there during the summer, since it was near one of their higher pastures. In the winter, they didn't use it as much—mainly as a resting place where they could warm up and dry out when they were out skiing.

Sterling had taken her skiing out in Devil's Glen on a couple of occasions in addition to the proposal night. From what he'd explained, they kept the cabin in good repair and well stocked with canned food, dried jerky, and coffee beans. They also had a supply of cut wood both inside and out to use as fuel in the stove.

Was the old cabin a place where she and Hyacinth could hide for a week or two, just until her father was forced to figure out another way to pay off his debts?

With the recent snowfall, they would likely need skis in order to reach the cabin, and neither she nor Hyacinth had skis. In fact, Hyacinth didn't know how to ski, and Violet only knew as much as Sterling had taught her last winter. But it was enough that she could get herself and Hyacinth there.

Violet crossed to the kitchen window that overlooked the garden, clothesline, and shed. The skis were stored in the shed, which was never locked.

She hesitated. They technically wouldn't be stealing the skis if they only intended to use them and then give them back. They also wouldn't be trespassing in the miner's cabin, since the Nobles often let people passing through the area use the place.

Besides, Sterling hadn't given them much choice. He'd said they had to be out of his house by dawn. The cabin was the best option.

She just hoped Sterling wouldn't realize the skis were missing and discover where they'd gone. Because if he did, she had no doubt he hated her enough that he'd kick her out of the cabin too.

Sterling stumbled out of bed, feeling as though he'd been run over by stampeding cattle.

A glance out the window told him that dawn was already breaking and morning light was creeping upon the ranch.

He hadn't meant to sleep so late, had only planned to rest for a couple of hours. But after the past nights of dealing with the sick cattle and getting so little rest, the sleep deprivation had caught up with him.

Still in the flannel shirt and denims he'd worn yesterday, he crossed from his bed to the door and didn't look into the mirror attached to the dresser. Every time he viewed himself there, it brought back memories of his wedding day, when he'd stood in his room with Maverick and had been getting ready, so full of excitement and hope.

Instead, Sterling combed his fingers through his hair,

grabbed his hat from the hook on the back of the door, and headed out, not even bothering with changing into fresh garments. He had no one to impress, especially not Violet.

He paused in the hallway and listened for any sounds coming from the kitchen, where he'd left Violet and Hyacinth.

Silence met him—the same silence that had been present since his family had left.

The women were being awfully quiet. They'd probably thrown down blankets in front of the stove and gone to sleep too.

Guilt pricked him, as it had when he'd left them and walked upstairs. He could have offered them his sisters' room for the night. He also hadn't needed to order them to be out before he came down.

He'd been trying to justify his callousness, telling himself Violet wouldn't leave anyway. She would probably plead for a ride back into town or maybe ask him for suggestions for where she could go next.

He started down the steps with a light tread so that he wouldn't wake them if they were still asleep.

Could he blame his unkindness on being tired? The surprise in seeing Violet again so unexpectedly? Regardless, he shouldn't have been a donkey's hind end. Especially if what she'd told him about her father was true.

Sterling hadn't wanted to believe her, didn't trust her. But what reason did she have to lie about why she was out in the middle of the night with Hyacinth? Why subject herself and Hyacinth to the elements? Why visit him when she hadn't bothered to respond to even one letter? Unless she was desperate.

As he reached the bottom of the stairs in the front hallway, he paused once more. Violet was here in his house.

His heartbeat stumbled forward. Not because he was anticipating seeing her again. No, all he was feeling was irritation that she'd sought him out. Really.

After running away from him and then closing herself off to any communication, she had a lot of nerve seeking him out now that she supposedly needed him. And her apology last night didn't mean anything. She'd given it in reaction to his putting her on the spot and calling out her selfishness. She wouldn't have apologized otherwise.

What exactly had she apologized for anyway? Certainly not for rejecting him or calling off their wedding. She apparently had no remorse for leaving him or losing him. She hadn't missed him or wished she'd stayed with him, had gone on with her life as if he hadn't meant anything to her.

No, she was only sorry she hadn't broken up with him in a kinder and gentler way.

He shook his head and forced down the pain that was

crowding into his chest.

This was why he hadn't wanted to see her again or be anywhere near her. Because just a few minutes in her presence was unearthing all the pain and heartache he'd worked so hard to overcome.

Scowling, he continued down the hallway, this time letting his footsteps echo loudly, hopefully warning the women he was coming and that he wasn't happy. He paused at the closed kitchen door, half tempted to push through without knocking. But as frustrated as he was, he wasn't an ogre. He wouldn't barge in on two women, not even in his own home.

He knocked. "Violet, I'm coming in."

Silence met him. From the absence of light coming from underneath the door, the women had turned out the lantern he'd left them. They were obviously asleep.

Should he let them slumber longer and come back later?

He pressed his hand against the door. Letting them stay another hour or two wouldn't hurt anything, would it?

He stuffed both hands into his pockets, slowly pivoted, then stopped.

Something was off. They should have heard his footsteps, at the very least his voice. What if she'd taken his instructions to be gone by dawn seriously after all? Had she left?

Without bothering to knock or call out another greeting, he pushed open the kitchen door. Even with only the faint light of dawn to illuminate the room, he could tell they weren't there.

He maneuvered to the worktable to light the lantern, only to discover it was gone.

Maybe they were using the outhouse.

He made his way to the back door and stepped outside onto the stoop. He scanned the yard, garden, shed, outhouse, and even the field beyond. Everything was dark with no sign of a lantern light.

Had they gone upstairs to one of the bedrooms?

With his pulse charging forward, he reentered the house, found another lantern and lit it, then made his way through each room. As he returned to the front hallway without a sign of them anywhere, a strange tension twisted through him.

He went to both barns and searched among the stalls and haylofts. After scouring every possible spot they could have gone, he halted in the ranch yard, the morning light softly cascading over mountains and glistening on the pine trees with their fresh layer of frost.

Violet had definitely taken his instructions to heart and departed from the ranch. "Good riddance," he whispered into the chilly morning air. But even as he spoke, the tension inside him only tightened.

The temperatures were still too cold for the women to

be outside for long. Violet wouldn't want Hyacinth to suffer again as she had last night. Did that mean she'd gone back home?

What if she'd been telling him the truth about her father wanting them to become dance girls at one of the saloons? It sounded too far-fetched to be even the least bit true. Not for a respectable man like Mr. Berkley. Even if he'd gotten into financial trouble due to gambling, he wasn't the sort of man who would subject his daughters to such degrading work.

On the other hand, what reason did Violet have for making up a story like that?

Sterling shifted his gaze toward the lane that led through the ranch and out to the main road to Breckenridge. He knew exactly how he could clear up the confusion. He would go directly to the Berkley residence and speak with Mr. Berkley about the matter.

Sterling blew out a breath of exasperation. Why was he allowing himself to care? Violet wasn't his problem. She'd chosen to end things with him. Let her figure out her life on her own.

But even as the bitter thoughts pushed to the front of his mind, his heart pulsed with the need to make sure she was okay. His pesky heart.

The truth was, he had always let his heart have too much importance...and look where that had gotten him in the past. Hadn't he learned that he couldn't let his heart dictate his decisions? Especially not with Violet.

Putting his head down, he forced himself to walk toward the cattle barn. He had dying cattle and his herd to save. He was too busy to worry about Violet. That was all there was to it.

She'd stolen from the Nobles. There was no getting around that fact.

Violet dragged her skis through the wet snow, the self-reproach of her thieving slowing her down. She'd also gone slower because Hyacinth was behind her and using skis for the first time.

Thankfully, her sister was a quick learner and had easily caught on to the sliding motion of the long wooden skis and the propelling effort with the wooden pole. Hyacinth hadn't complained once over the past couple of hours of traveling. Of course, they'd had to stop occasionally for breaks, especially because their bags were burdensome. But they'd managed to have some fun skiing down a few of the hills, allowing the momentum to take them faster.

Now, from the widening of the pastureland ahead, Violet recognized the area along the creek and knew they were getting close to the miner's cabin. They finally had full daylight, with sunlight against the snow almost blinding them. They certainly no longer needed the lantern she'd taken.

Yes, she'd stolen the lantern, matches, and food. At the time, when she'd been stuffing the few staples into their bags, she had justified her actions, mollifying herself with the assurance that Sterling and the whole Noble family would offer her the goods if they could understand the desperation of her situation.

As it was, Sterling hadn't believed her and hadn't cared even the slightest about her predicament. She should have known that would be the outcome of her visit, that he would hate her with as much passion as he'd once loved her.

A part of her had obviously been in denial over how much she'd hurt him. She'd been going about her life and focusing on her own problems without considering the depth of his feelings and his reaction to all that had happened.

With a huff of frustration at herself, Violet dug her pole into the snow and slid forward, first on one ski, then the next, before lifting her pole and repeating the motions, edging closer to the creek. At least the morning was clear, and although the air was frigid, her limbs and toes and fingers weren't quite as cold as they'd been last night, probably because the trek had been strenuous enough that, at times, perspiration had formed on her brow.

If only she'd been able to leave Noble Ranch without taking anything beyond the skis. But the need to save herself and Hyacinth had taken precedence.

Even these hours later, after hearing her father's acquiescence to Claude's plan, Violet couldn't grasp just how deplorable it was that the man who claimed to love his daughters had so readily given them over to another man.

Had Father always been so weak? Or had he become that way after Mother had left him? Because wasn't that what had happened?—she'd finally had her fill of Father's gambling and decided to leave him to his own fate. Maybe she'd been waiting for an excuse to go, and the failed wedding had provided her one.

Whatever the case, Mother had packed her bags and never once looked back, never once talked of returning, and never once mentioned their father. It was as if she'd wanted to put him out of their lives totally and completely. Perhaps she'd thought she had. She probably hadn't told Father where they were or what they were doing.

He'd been cut from their lives until Violet had sent him the telegram letting him know about Mother's death.

Violet released another breath, a white cloud filling the air in front of her. She shouldn't have contacted him.

If she'd had any sense about her, she would have realized Mother had taken them far away from Father to protect them. But she'd been too trusting, too gullible, too easily swayed by Father's promise to take care of them, and instead of staying away, she'd walked right back into his chaotic life and gotten tangled in his mess.

Running away to this cabin was their last option to try to break free from him.

"I'll pay the Nobles back," she whispered. "I vow it." Someday, when she had her own interior designing business, she might have enough income to cover the expenses. Until then, she could only add the stealing to the list of transgressions she'd committed against Sterling and his family.

She slowed her skis and searched among the pine trees across the frozen creek. The blanket of snow on the branches was pristine, as fresh and untouched as it had been the few other times she'd been here.

Where was the cabin? Had she taken a wrong path at some point? She'd thought she knew the general route into Devil's Glen. But what if she'd been overconfident?

"There!" came Hyacinth's breathy call from behind her. "I see a cabin."

Violet peered in the direction of her sister's outstretched mittened hand. The woodland ahead blocked the view, but tucked away in a sheltered nook, the log structure was a welcome sight.

"That's it." Violet pushed forward again, relief giving her a burst of energy. She was a city girl and didn't know much about surviving in a cabin away from civilization. But they were also young and resourceful. They'd do just fine. At least, she prayed they would.

As she reached the embankment that led to the creek, she lifted her pole and pointed her skis down. She leaned forward and let the slick snow carry her faster. With the cold air slapping at her cheeks, she almost smiled at the memories of skiing with Sterling, how he'd stayed right beside her, watching over her and teaching her so patiently. The times skiing together had always been enjoyable. Because of the skiing? Or because she'd been with him?

The bottom of the hill came too quickly, and she turned her skis sideways to stop as Sterling had taught her. But in the next instant, her ski hit something buried beneath the snow. While one ski twisted the way she'd planned, the other went the opposite direction.

The shift happened too fast to stop, and a sharp pain ricocheted through her ankle, as if her foot were being wrenched from her body. Her leg buckled beneath her, unable to bear her weight. Even though she tried to hold herself up with her ski pole, she found herself tumbling down and tossing her bag aside.

The fall only bent her ankle all the more, and she cried out, grabbing her foot, trying to unbuckle her boot from the ski and free herself from the agonizing position.

"What's wrong, Vi?" Cheeks flushed from the cold, Hyacinth came to a halt beside her, her eyes wide and filled with concern.

Violet couldn't speak past the pain and clawed at her boot, needing to free her foot.

In the next instant, Hyacinth was bending down and helping her, obviously seeing the problem. She worked calmly and methodically, loosening the buckles. As she shifted the boot off the ski, the burning shot through Violet's ankle again.

"Careful." Violet grasped the area and tried to draw in a breath. "It's hurt. Badly."

Hyacinth gentled her touch, lifting Violet's foot more carefully. "Does it feel broken?"

"I don't know how to tell."

Hyacinth brushed her fingers lightly along Violet's stocking and then across her boot. "It's swelling already."

Violet's whole leg was beginning to throb, and she felt suddenly weak, almost sick to her stomach.

Her sister glanced in the direction of the cabin, still at least two hundred feet away, across the creek and surrounded by trees. "We need to get to the cabin and take your boot off."

Hyacinth unbuckled the other ski, then Violet tried to push up while Hyacinth assisted her. As Violet finally stood on one leg with Hyacinth bracing her up, the dizziness and pain were almost too much to bear.

"I can't move." Violet couldn't imagine even standing on her foot, much less walking the rest of the distance. As deep as the snow was, she'd never make it by favoring her good leg, not even if Hyacinth helped bear her weight.

Hyacinth peered around. She'd discarded her hood, probably from the exertion of their trip. Her dark hair was in a single braid like Violet's, and strands had come loose, brushing her cheeks. At the moment, she'd never looked more beautiful. And innocent.

A surge of protectiveness swelled within Violet again. Father was a monster for even thinking about giving Hyacinth over to men who would pay to hold her, manhandle her, and lust over her.

Hyacinth cocked her head at the low branches of a nearby spruce. "I'll break off a limb or two. You can get on like a sled, and I'll pull you the distance to the cabin."

Would that work? They had to give it a try.

Hyacinth helped Violet sit down. Then she maneuvered on her skis toward the nearest tree.

Violet could only recline in the snow, gritting her teeth through the pain. If her ankle was broken, what would she do? How would she ever be able to travel the two hours or more to town to reach a doctor? She would never consider sending Hyacinth back for the doctor on her own.

Would they be trapped at the cabin? How long could

they stay before their food supply ran out?

Violet shifted, and pain shot through her leg and up her body. A groan slipped out before she could stop it.

Hyacinth, nearly at the tree, halted and peered back with a creased brow. "Hang in there, Vi. I'll take care of you."

All Violet could manage was a nod.

While her sister wrestled to break the lowest branches off the spruce tree, Violet could feel her body temperature dropping as the cold and dampness from the snow began to creep through the layers of her clothing.

It seemed like ages but was probably only a few minutes before Hyacinth was returning, dragging two large pine boughs. Somehow, with Hyacinth's help, Violet managed to crawl onto the branches.

Leaving their luggage behind for Hyacinth to retrieve later, they inched toward the cabin, Hyacinth trying to make the ride smooth. Even so, each movement jarred Violet so that by the time they were across the frozen creek, she couldn't hold back her whimpers.

When they finally reached the cabin, Hyacinth collapsed in front of the door, her breath coming in gasps. Violet could only lie on the boughs and stare up at the sky, the tears silently coursing down her cheeks, leaving an icy trail in their wake.

What had she gotten them into? And how would they ever survive?

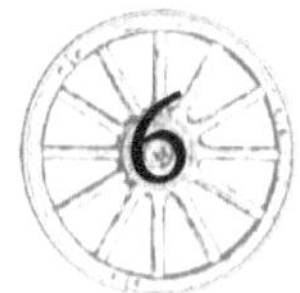

He was probably the world's weakest man.

If not, why was he standing at the front door of the Berkley home?

Sterling lifted a hand to knock but then stuffed his hand into his coat pocket.

What was he doing here?

He stared at the simple two-story structure that was only a couple of years old, painted white, with a small yard that was overgrown and in much need of manicuring since the last time he'd visited. When had that been? In April before the wedding?

Back then, he'd gone to town a couple of evenings a week to call on Violet. When the weather had permitted, they'd strolled outside. The other times, they'd visited in the parlor while her mother and sister sat on the opposite side of the room, embroidering or sewing and pretending not to pay attention to him and Violet.

Their courtship hadn't lasted long, perhaps six months, maybe nine, before he'd proposed marriage to her. That had been plenty long enough for him. He'd assumed she'd had enough time too.

But somehow, he'd been wrong about everything.

So what was he doing back at her house? Why was he getting himself involved with Violet again?

He shifted his attention to the hitching post where he'd tied his horse. He shouldn't be here. He needed to ride out of town as fast as he could, back to the ranch.

With an exasperated breath, he pivoted to go. But the moment he did so, he took in the storm clouds that were forming above the mountains in the west. At midday, the sun overhead was starting to warm the air, but from the looks of things, the high country would get more snow before the day was out.

He only had to picture Violet and Hyacinth as they'd looked last night on his porch, cold and tired and scared. He didn't want to think of them out another night, especially if it were snowing.

As much as he'd tried to deny Violet's claim about being in trouble, deep inside, he knew she was right. Even if he wished she hadn't come to him for help, she had. Now he might be the only one who could do something for the two women.

Besides, if he rode back to the ranch, he'd only drive himself crazy like he had all morning, wondering where the women had gone and if they were safe. He'd tried to focus on his meeting with Thatcher and come up with a plan to vaccinate the herd against blackleg. He'd fed the cattle in the pasture, broken ice for them to drink, separated out any others that looked sick. But through it all, he hadn't been able to stop worrying about Violet.

He hated himself for how weak he was when it came to her, hated that she could fill his head so completely again, hated that he couldn't remain indifferent toward her, hated that he cared what was going on in her life, hated that he didn't want her to be in danger.

He dropped his head, disgusted with himself. He was only asking for more pain and heartache by getting involved in her life again. But what else could he do?

He tipped the brim of his hat lower to shield his eyes from the bright rays of the sun. Then he forced himself to turn back around and knocked on the door with several firm raps.

He might be the world's weakest man, but he couldn't leave until he talked to Mr. Berkley and was reassured that Violet and Hyacinth had someplace to live and weren't in danger of having to work at the dancehall.

He waited, listening for footsteps inside or any sign that someone was coming to the door.

Only silence greeted him.

He lifted a hand and pounded against the door again, this time louder, before stepping back and scanning the windows. The curtain in the parlor shifted. Someone—maybe Violet—was there but perhaps was too afraid to answer the door. Maybe she hadn't seen his approach and was using caution.

"Violet." He leaned closer to the door, hoping his voice would carry to the parlor. "It's me, Sterling."

He waited quietly.

A moment later, footsteps echoed in the hallway. They were too heavy and halting to belong to Violet.

The lock on the other side rattled, and the door opened to reveal Mr. Berkley standing on the threshold. With a receding hairline and spectacles, Violet's father had always looked scholarly and gentlemanly. But today he wasn't wearing a coat or vest. His shirt was wrinkled and untucked with stains streaking the front. He wore one suspender to keep his trousers up, and the other dangled down his leg.

Something was definitely wrong.

"Sterling?" Mr. Berkley's eyes were bloodshot and his face in need of a shave. Even his hair, which had always been so neatly trimmed, needed a cut. His forehead was grooved with creases, making him appear ten years older than the last time Sterling had seen him, the day of the wedding.

"Mr. Berkley." Sterling peered beyond the man, hoping for a glimpse of Violet so that he could reassure himself she'd come home and hadn't run off somewhere else. The signs of her were everywhere—the tall vases with the dried floral arrangements, the artfully arranged decorations on the side table, the elegant rug that matched her color scheme.

She'd loved to decorate, was actually quite talented at it, claimed she'd learned her trade from her mother after moving so often over the years and having to decorate each new house. During their courtship, Violet had shyly admitted that she hoped one day to have a house-decorating business of her own. And of course, he'd told her he couldn't wait for her to decorate their house—the house he'd been saving to build for her.

"Can I help you?" Mr. Berkley's gaze darted up and down the street before he shrank back, but not before Sterling glimpsed the fear in his eyes.

Maybe the fellow really was in trouble from gambling, which was strange, because Mr. Berkley had never struck Sterling as a gambler, unless he'd started gaming after his wife and daughters had gone east.

"I came to check on Violet. Wanted to make sure she's okay."

"I'm sorry." Mr. Berkley began to close the door. "She's not home right now."

"She's not?" Sterling shot out a hand and braced it against the door to hold it open. "Do you know where she went?"

"I imagine she's out running errands."

"So she returned home?"

"Returned?" Mr. Berkley's eyes widened, revealing hopefulness. "Have you seen her today?"

A warning rang inside Sterling. If Violet had come to him in secret in the middle of the night, that probably meant she didn't want her father knowing her whereabouts, and that included her trip out to his ranch. "No, I haven't seen her today." That was the truth, even if it wasn't the whole truth.

"Oh." Mr. Berkley's shoulders sagged. "So you don't know where she is?"

Sterling hesitated. He had to say something to Mr. Berkley about the dancehall. But he had to do so carefully, in a way that didn't make things worse for Violet.

"Listen, Mr. Berkley. I know about the dancehall job you want Violet and Hyacinth to take."

"Then you have seen my daughters, haven't you?"

Disappointment sifted through Sterling. He'd hoped Mr. Berkley would angrily step forward and declare he'd never consider having his daughters work in a dancehall. But his lack of denial told Sterling that everything Violet had spoken about her father was true.

"Where are they?" the middle-aged man persisted. "At your ranch?"

"Why would I be here looking for Violet if she was at my ranch?" He had to throw the man off Violet's trail any way he could.

Mr. Berkley's gaze once again darted to the street both ways, a wildness in his expression. The fellow was obviously in trouble for his gambling debts.

Sterling couldn't formulate an ounce of pity. Instead, only anger burned through him. What kind of father would sell his daughters to a saloon in order to save himself from ruin? A coward of a father, that's what.

Sterling straightened his shoulders and then leveled his most severe glare upon the man. "You're despicable." He spat the words. "Trying to force your daughters to pay for your debt, your problems."

Mr. Berkley took a rapid step back. "I'm not—"

"Don't come near Violet or Hyacinth again." Sterling didn't realize he'd shifted his coat aside and gripped the handle of his revolver until Mr. Berkley's gaze slid there. "Stay away from them, do you hear me?"

Mr. Berkley seemed to swallow hard. "I don't have a choice about them working at the dancehall. I shook on the deal with Claude."

"Unshake the deal."

"I can't. I signed the offer this morning."

"I don't care if you signed a note in blood." Sterling's voice rose with his anger. "You resolve your own problems like a man instead of cowering behind your daughters."

Mr. Berkley had the decency to finally look

chagrined. With a shaking hand, he tugged at one of the undone buttons on his shirt. "Maybe you can loan me the money, Sterling. For old times' sake."

Sterling didn't know the amount Mr. Berkley owed but guessed it was substantial if he was in trouble enough that he'd sell out his own daughters.

"Please, Sterling. I promise I'll repay you." Mr. Berkley grabbed Sterling's arm, revealing overlong fingernails that were lined with grime.

What had happened to bring him to this point?

Something in the man's expression told Sterling that owing gambling debts wasn't a new problem, that he had a history of the trouble.

If so, why hadn't Violet ever told him about her father's issues?

Sterling had the feeling the story was complex, had even been embarrassing. Even so, that didn't excuse her for not telling him. Was it possible he'd never given her the opportunity to be open? Had he been so enamored with her that he'd glossed over deeper issues? Had he pushed them too fast and, in doing so, neglected having more meaningful conversations?

A strange tremor worked through his chest. All this time he'd been blaming Violet for ruining their relationship. What if he'd had some responsibility in the demise too? What if he'd played a much greater role than he'd realized?

Had he done something to unknowingly push her away? He hadn't thought about that possibility before. Even if his actions hadn't alienated her, he had to admit he hadn't facilitated openness with her. If he had, wouldn't she have felt more comfortable coming to him and talking about what was wrong instead of running away and hiding all that she felt?

Sterling stared at Mr. Berkley for a moment longer, the tremor spreading throughout his body. Yes, he'd been blaming her for everything and hadn't considered how he may have been insensitive or callous to her.

"If you loan me the money," Mr. Berkley said, the desperation back in his voice, "I'll make sure Violet marries you this time."

Sterling shook his head. "No. I don't want Violet back, especially not like that." Like a piece of livestock going to the highest bidder. "The truth is, you'll have to figure out how to pay off your debts on your own, without my help, and definitely without Violet's."

Mr. Berkley's shoulders slumped. "Of course. You're right. You're right."

"Then you agree that pressuring your daughters to work at the dancehall is despicable?"

Mr. Berkley nodded, almost sadly. "Yes, it's quite despicable. And I shouldn't have agreed to it."

"That's right." Sterling prayed the man was sincere. "You'll call off the deal?"

"I have to. It's not fair to my daughters."

"You need to rip up that offer."

"Of course."

"Good." Sterling released a tight breath, the tension starting to ease from his muscles. Maybe he was helping Violet today by getting Mr. Berkley to recognize the error of his ways. Hopefully, now she would be able to return home and be safe.

He still wasn't sure where she'd gone off to. But once he tracked her down, he'd reassure her that her father was apologetic and wouldn't hand her over to anyone in a scheme to pay off his debt.

Without another word to Mr. Berkley, Sterling turned and made his way back to his horse.

The clouds gathering in the west were turning darker and more ominous. Where had Violet gone? That was the bigger issue at the moment, especially with snow on the way. The other issue was whether or not he ought to keep looking for her or let her go.

Certainly, after coming to town, he'd done more than his fair share. It was time to get back to work and put her from his mind.

Sterling tried to stick to his resolve. Once he was home, he kept busy. But he couldn't lock his thoughts of her away. They refused to be contained. By mid-afternoon, he explained the situation to Beckett and sent him into town to find out who Claude was. Sterling had wanted to go himself but knew he'd only raise suspicions if he went to town twice in one day.

Beckett was all too willing to go since he was expecting a letter from his mail-order bride.

All the while the ranch foreman was gone, Sterling's mind wouldn't rest, and his worry over Violet wouldn't go away, especially as the clouds blew in and snow began to fall.

When Beckett finally returned in the late afternoon, Sterling met him in the ranch yard, which was covered in at least an inch of fresh snow, with flakes still falling fast and the sky growing steadily darker.

"Is she home yet?" Sterling didn't waste time with a greeting.

"Hello to you too." Beckett removed his hat and thumped it against his leg to dislodge the snow. Then he slapped it back on and gave Sterling a stern look. "Yep, I'm fine. Thanks for asking."

Sterling didn't care if Beckett was assuming he still cared about Violet. He supposed it did look like he was obsessed with her today. But he was only doing what any God-fearing and kindhearted man would do. He was helping the less fortunate.

"Did you find her?" Sterling persisted.

"No one's seen a hair of Violet or her sister all day."

"What about Claude?" Sterling fired off the question. "Who's he?"

"He owns the Red Cap Saloon."

Sterling had never heard of it. Then again, he didn't go to town often and had lost count of all the new saloons that had opened over the past couple of years. "What else?"

"Apparently, he's got a big place with several gaming rooms at the back of his saloon."

"And he has dance girls?"

Beckett's expression hardened. "He's got just about any kind of woman you could want, if you get my meaning."

Sterling silently cursed. He didn't want Violet or Hyacinth anywhere near such a place.

"Heard this Claude's a nice fellow until he gets crossed. Then he gets meaner than a bobcat in a gunny sack."

That wasn't good news for Mr. Berkley. But the fellow would have to work things out with Claude without involving Violet and Hyacinth. That's all there was to it.

Still in his saddle and covered in snow, Beckett opened the flap of his saddlebag. He pulled out a package wrapped in brown paper and tossed it to Sterling.

Sterling caught it.

"From Clementine." Beckett nudged his horse toward the barn. "She said it's your favorite."

Sterling sniffed the bundle, catching a whiff of the

rich scent of chocolate and pecans with caramel.

Clementine was the little sister of his best friend Maverick Oakley. She'd just married the livery owner, Grady Worth, and had opened her own candy shop.

"Said you might need some cheering up."

"Why?"

Beckett snorted. "Reckon everyone thinks you're going crazy now that Violet's back in town."

"I'm fine." He ground out the words.

"Course you're not going crazy," Beckett called over his shoulder with an eye roll. "Not at all."

Sterling huffed, the white puff mingling with large snowflakes. Okay, maybe he was going slightly crazy.

He crossed through the fresh snow to the house to put the candy away. Was he also hoping Violet would be back?

As he entered the quiet house, he expelled a frustrated breath, knowing she wasn't there and that he shouldn't be wishing she'd show up again. Regardless, he made his way into the kitchen, lit a lantern, and added more fuel to the kitchen stove.

He opened the candy from Clementine and sank his teeth into one of the delicacies. With the coming of evening, he missed his family and their meals in the dining room together. Since he was alone, he'd taken to eating at the bunkhouse with the men. In fact, he didn't have much food in the house. Just a few staples in the hutch.

His gaze drifted to the shelf, and he paused his chewing. Empty.

What had happened to the coffee beans, molasses, crackers, lard, and flour?

Had Violet and Hyacinth taken the food? What other explanation was there?

Of course, he hadn't noticed when he'd come into the kitchen earlier in the day, because he'd been too focused on trying to find the women. But now there was no missing the fact that the two had helped themselves to the food.

Why? Because they had a place to go? Somewhere they could cook their own meals?

His mind spun with the implications. Were there any homes in the area that were sitting empty?

The little piece of land with the strawberry farm that Clarabelle Oakley—now Clarabelle Meyer—owned was being rented to Thatcher Hoyt. Thankfully it was only a couple of miles away, because they needed a veterinarian now more than ever before.

There weren't any vacant homesteads or houses in the area that Sterling knew about. Unless Violet had heard of one that he hadn't.

"Where did you go, Violet?" he whispered into the silent kitchen as melting snow dripped from his boots and coat.

She wouldn't have been able to go too far without a

way to get around. Unless…

Sterling stalked across the kitchen, out the back door, and made a direct line for the shed. The flakes hit his face, and a cold breeze tried to slither down the collar of his coat. He stopped at the shed, tossed open the door, and peered at the wall where he kept the skis, half a dozen pairs lined up by size.

His pulse leaped. Even in the dim lighting, he could see that two of the spots were empty. Two of the shorter pairs that his sisters had always worn were gone.

Victoria and Hyacinth had taken the food and the skis.

He'd gone skiing with Violet last winter, had taught her how to navigate in the snowy foothills and even how to ride the slopes downhill. In fact, the day he'd proposed to her, they'd skied out to the miner's cabin…

His thoughts came to a crashing halt. Was that where she'd headed?

It had to be. She knew the way well enough. And it wasn't too far.

He let his body sag with relief. He'd solved the mystery of her disappearance finally.

A gust of frigid air hit him in the back and nearly knocked his hat from his head. At the same moment, it sent an icy warning through him.

The way to the cabin often became impassable for weeks at a time after particularly heavy snowfalls, which meant Violet and Hyacinth could end up trapped there. Even after some melting, the trails were still difficult for even the most experienced skiers such as himself. If the women had any problems or ran short on fuel or food, they would attempt to leave, which could end up being deadly.

He had to get to them before that happened.

He glanced over his shoulder to the sky and the falling snow. Darkness was creeping upon the ranch, and the snow didn't show any signs of letting up. If he had any chance of reaching the cabin tonight, he had to leave right away. Doing so would be risky, especially since the wind seemed to be picking up. He might find himself in the middle of a blizzard in the dark and could take a wrong turn, lose his way, get hurt…or worse.

With a shake of his head, he stepped into the shed and reached for his skis. No matter the danger to himself, he was going after the women right away.

Violet huddled against Hyacinth in the bottom bunk bed. They'd piled on every blanket they could find and curled up together. However, they were still cold, since they hadn't been able to start a fire in the stove, and the temperature in the cabin had gotten colder, especially once the storm had blown in, bringing snow and wind.

Violet pinched her eyes closed as if that could somehow make all their problems disappear. But the pain in her swollen and bruised ankle was the constant reminder that their current situation was all too real. The chill in the air was the other reminder of how dangerous their predicament was and that it soon could become life-threatening.

She shuddered, only to have Hyacinth, in front of her, squeeze her arms tighter.

"You're still awake?" Violet asked.

"I am." Wearing her coat and layers of clothes and

boots, Hyacinth was heavily bundled, just like Violet.

"Try to sleep," Violet said softly. They'd gotten so little sleep last night, and they were both exhausted.

"You do know I'll have to leave in the morning and go for help."

"No, absolutely not." Violet didn't want to think about sending Hyacinth out into a snowy wilderness by herself. Too many things that could go wrong already had, and she didn't want to take any more risks.

Hyacinth seemed about to protest, then expelled a breath. "I suppose there's no sense in fighting about it since we'll probably be snowed in by morning."

They lay quietly for a moment, the wind rattling the windows and even the roof, as if agreeing with Hyacinth.

"I'm sorry," Violet whispered. "We shouldn't have come out here."

"You were only trying to save us."

"But now look. We're in worse trouble."

"I'd rather die here than dance in a saloon with strangers."

Violet didn't want to say that there was a very good chance they could die out here without heat.

If only they'd been more careful with the few remaining matches in the cabin when they'd been trying to start a fire. But they'd quickly used them up in their futile efforts, not worrying because they had more in their bags.

Violet blamed herself for the mistake. She'd been in so much pain by the time she'd reached the cabin that she hadn't been thinking straight. They'd been in a hurry to get her boot off and tend to her ankle. Hyacinth had always been the more medically minded of the two of them and had elevated Violet's leg and then made a cold compress out of snow to try to reduce the swelling.

By then, heavy, wet snowflakes had been falling. When Hyacinth had gone back to get their valises, everything had been snow-covered and damp. They hadn't realized the matches they'd brought along had gotten wet until too late. By that point, it had been snowing too hard to attempt to return to the ranch.

So they'd resolved to get through the night. Somehow. Violet could only pray that in the morning, her ankle would feel better, the weather would be clear, and they would both be able to leave together.

At least the cabin was sturdy and the chinking solid. It had two sets of bunk beds with flimsy mattresses held by box frames. A long table with benches took up most of the rest of the room, with a rusty old stove in the corner along with two scuffed chairs.

A couple of large trunks contained supplies—one with linens, blankets, towels, and soap, and the other with the few matches they'd used up and some canned foods—although not as much as Violet remembered from the last time she'd been here.

She winced as she moved her foot, which was too swollen to fit back into her boot. "We'll have to go back to the Noble Ranch."

"No." Hyacinth's response was filled with loathing. "After the way Sterling treated us, I refuse to go there."

"It's the closest place."

"I don't mind traveling farther to get help."

"We might not be able to make it farther." Violet didn't exactly want to see Sterling ever again either. She'd already humiliated herself enough with him last night. Of course, she deserved every bit of his bitterness and scorn toward her. But she had expected a little more kindness and concern. Maybe even some fondness. After all, he'd once declared his love so ardently. If he'd truly loved her as much as he'd professed, how could all of that love disappear? Unless it had never really been as deep as he'd made it seem.

Wasn't that the way it had been with her father too? He claimed to love her and Hyacinth. But when difficulties arose, his love wasn't reliable.

Hyacinth released a mirthless laugh. "I hope you weren't thinking that you would get back together with Sterling."

"No, that hadn't crossed my mind at all." She could admit that during the carriage ride up the pass to Breckenridge, she had thought about him—what he was doing, how he was faring, and if he'd moved on with another woman. She'd wondered what it would be like to see him in passing, how he would act toward her, what he would say.

Well, she didn't need to guess any longer. He couldn't stand being in the same room with her—so much so that he'd hardly even looked at her or talked to her.

Another gust of wind shook the cabin, sending a whistle down the stovepipe and rattling the hollow metal tubes.

If only Mother hadn't died. She'd been their solid rock amidst the chaos that Father had always brought to their lives.

At a thud against the door, Violet's eyes flew open to darkness—because, of course, they hadn't been able to light the lantern either.

Hyacinth stiffened, while Violet pushed up to her elbow and stared through the dark in the direction of the door. Was someone there, or had the wind blown a branch or icicle against the cabin?

The door rattled harder. "Open up, Violet," came a muffled voice.

She sat up all the way, her heartbeat racing. Who was it, and how had the person known she was here?

Hyacinth thrust off the covers and sat on the edge of the bed.

"It's me. Sterling."

A strange wave of emotion rushed through Violet, making her weak and sending tears to the backs of her eyes. Sterling had come after her. The good and decent man she'd gotten to know last year was still there inside him after all.

She blinked hard to keep the tears from flooding her eyes, then she nudged her sister. "Go let him in."

Hyacinth didn't move. "I despise him."

"We need him. And he came all this way to help us." She knew it deep in her heart.

Hyacinth scooted forward but hesitated.

The pounding on the door grew louder.

Violet pushed her sister again, and this time Hyacinth rose and shuffled forward slowly. A moment later, Violet could hear her jiggling the lock. As the door swung open, light filled the cabin along with swirling snow.

Sterling shook the snow from his coat and hat, then stepped inside and shut the door. He locked it before turning and lifting the lantern so that the light spilled across the cabin, revealing Hyacinth standing by the table, glaring at him.

Sterling examined her quickly before scanning the rest of the cabin. His gaze was almost frantic until it landed upon Violet in the bed. As he took her in, some of the tension seemed to ease from his face.

Once again that strange emotion welled inside her. Maybe he did still care about her more than he'd let on.

At the very least, he was a decent man who was willing to help her during her moment of trouble.

She wanted to sit up and prove to him she was capable and dependent and just fine. But she couldn't get her injured leg to move, so she remained motionless. "Hi, Sterling."

He didn't respond. Instead, his gaze went to the unheated stove and the pile of damp matches on the floor beside it. He hung the lantern on a hook in the beam above the table, then he shed his mittens, dug in his pocket, and produced a match.

Grabbing a handful of shavings from the wood box, he opened the stove door and set to work adding kindling to the small pile Hyacinth had formed earlier. Within seconds, he had a blaze going, then he continued to add wood from the stack beside the door.

Hyacinth had edged closer to the warmth but held herself stiffly away from Sterling.

When finally the flames were crackling high, Sterling stood, glanced at Violet, and motioned toward the stove. "Come get warmed up."

Embarrassment pulsed through her. She didn't want Sterling to know how utterly helpless she was and how she'd gotten into an impossible situation. So she did the first thing she could think of. She changed the subject. "How did you know we were here?"

"I saw the missing food and skis."

She should have guessed she couldn't get anything past Sterling. "I'm surprised you braved the storm to travel here."

He took off his hat, then he nodded at the stove again. "Come on. You need to warm up."

"Don't misunderstand me. I'm grateful you came, since we had no dry matches left. But you took a big risk heading up here in this storm."

"It's a good thing I did." His eyes were dark and filled with frustration.

She wrapped the blankets tighter around her. "We would have been fine for one night."

"Do you think you could have skied out of here tomorrow?"

"Maybe." Probably not. But she wouldn't admit that to him.

He shook his head, his expression grave. "I barely made it here. There's no way we'll make it out tomorrow."

She didn't quite know how to respond. One way or another, she and Hyacinth probably would have frozen to death if Sterling hadn't come after them.

As he held her gaze, the seriousness in his eyes only confirmed the danger.

A shiver raced up her spine.

He pulled a bench closer to the fire. "Sit here."

She tried to move her leg again but winced.

"What's wrong?" His voice was sharp.

"I'm fine—"

"She injured her ankle." Hyacinth spoke at the same time as Violet.

Sterling's boots clomped across the puncheon log floor. He was beside her in the next instant, shoving aside the blankets on her legs.

She jerked the cover back down. "Hyacinth has taken care of it."

"Let me see it," he growled.

"There's nothing you can do."

He shot her a fierce scowl, then tugged aside the blanket again. His eyes dared her to defy him, and the stubborn set of his jaw told her he wouldn't be swayed from examining her.

She sighed and leaned back.

He lowered himself to his knees and tenderly peeled back the towels she'd wrapped around her ankle and foot for warmth. As the covering fell away to reveal the discolored and swollen skin that circled her ankle, his brows pinched together.

He pressed his fingers against the puffy areas. "Tell me where it hurts the most."

"Everywhere."

He tossed her a censuring look, one that told her to cooperate.

As he probed near the inside of her ankle, the pain

was sharp. "There. That hurt."

He gentled his touch and continued to assess her. When he finished, he lowered her foot to the mattress. "I've seen broken ankles, and yours seems more like a sprain than a fracture."

"Let's hope you're right."

He covered her foot up, then sat back on his heels and glanced around the cabin, pursing his lips as he did when he was coming up with a plan.

How was it that she could remember what his various facial expressions meant? She'd never been able to forget his smile. It turned the brown of his eyes almost golden and made his eyes crinkle at the corners. It also relaxed his features and the hardness of his jaw so that he was less intimidating.

She'd been able to bring out his smile from time to time when they'd been courting, and she'd loved being able to do so.

He stood, shed his coat, then before she knew what he was doing, he reached down and slid his arms beneath her, lifting her off the bed.

"Sterling, put me down."

Ignoring her, he straightened, his movements cautious. As he turned and started toward the stove, he cocked his head toward one of the two chairs in the cabin. "Move the chairs closer to the fire," he said to Hyacinth.

The young woman lifted her chin at Sterling as

though she might defy him, then with a glare that held her contempt, she dragged the chairs directly in front of the stove.

With Sterling's face so close, Violet couldn't keep from studying his features, chiseled and bronzed and weathered. The layer of dark scruff only added to his ruggedness. He was every bit as attractive now as he'd been the day she'd first seen him. Of course, her body reacted as it always had, with a flutter low in her abdomen.

There was no questioning how handsome Sterling Noble was. He was one of the best-looking men in the area.

No, her physical attraction to him had never been the issue. She could admit that she'd liked holding his hand when they'd walked, had loved being in his arms when they'd hugged, and had felt a liquid heat when they'd kissed. While they hadn't kissed often, they had kissed a few times as their wedding day had approached.

Even though the physical magnetism had grown between them, he'd been a strong man of character and had remained respectful with her. She could appreciate that more now than she had at the time. A lesser man might have pushed for more, especially so close to their wedding. But not Sterling. He'd remained in control of himself and had always treated her with the utmost respect.

So why had she run away from him when he was not only attractive but also a man of such high character?

That question had nagged her for the past months. Of course, her first and main excuse had always been her uncertainty about loving him enough to marry him. She'd cared about him deeply, but she'd had too many doubts about whether she was ready to commit to him forever.

But if lack of love had been the only reason for her unsettled feelings during those days leading up to the wedding, then why hadn't she just told Sterling she needed more time and postponed the wedding instead of running away?

On one hand, she had told Sterling she was feeling rushed, and that was why she'd turned down his first proposal right in this cabin. On the other hand, maybe she hadn't communicated her hesitancy well enough. If she'd been more direct and told him she wanted to court longer, would he have listened? Or would he have been upset at her anyway?

Whatever the case, she hadn't resolved her issues by running away from the wedding, and she wasn't sure she ever would understand what had happened. But now that she'd crossed paths with Sterling again, a part of her wanted to figure out why she'd thrown away a relationship with a man like him.

As he reached one of the chairs, he used his foot to position it. Then he lowered her as if she were a breakable heirloom, one he couldn't bear to part with. Which wasn't the truth. Maybe once upon a time he hadn't wanted to part ways with her, but last night he hadn't been able to get away from her fast enough.

When he lowered her to the chair, he didn't linger. Instead, he held her legs, dragged the other chair closer, then positioned her feet on it. He rolled up a blanket and positioned it under her foot, elevating it more.

"There." He stood back and took her in. "That should help."

She was wearing only one stocking, and her injured foot was bare. Her skirt had slipped forward almost to her knee, revealing not only her discolored and swollen ankle but also her calf. The showing of her leg was indecent, and she wanted to tug down her skirt.

But she forced herself to remain motionless. Of course Sterling wasn't thinking about her bare leg at a time like this. He was focused on helping her bring down the swelling in her ankle. That was all.

"You'll sleep in the chair tonight, and that should help ease the pain." He towered above her, concern lines etched into his forehead.

She wanted to offer him a grateful smile, but his eyes were still guarded, even if they were no longer filled with loathing. "Thank you, Sterling—"

"If she falls asleep," Hyacinth interrupted, hovering beside her, "she might topple out of the chair."

"She won't fall." Sterling situated a bench beside Violet.

"She very well could."

"I'll be watching her."

Hyacinth fisted her hands on her hips, disapproval radiating from her taut frame. Sterling just glared back at her.

"I'll be fine." Violet offered her sister a reassuring smile. "Now that Sterling is here and we have warmth, we'll both rest easier."

Hyacinth took a few more moments to warm herself by the fire, then yawned and crossed back to the bunk bed. The cabin was already much warmer than it had been only ten minutes previously, and it would continue to get warm now that the fire was blazing.

Hyacinth divided up the blankets into three piles, but Sterling refused to take any. She didn't argue with him and gave Violet two extra and took a couple for herself. Hyacinth was asleep in minutes, and Violet could feel her eyes closing too.

She could hear Sterling heating water and adding more fuel to the stove. She wouldn't mind having some quiet moments to talk to him and try to apologize again. But now that she was safe and warm, all her worries seemed to fade into nothing. She was strangely content with Sterling so close, knowing he would keep her and Hyacinth safe. Before she could ask him a question, she felt herself drifting off.

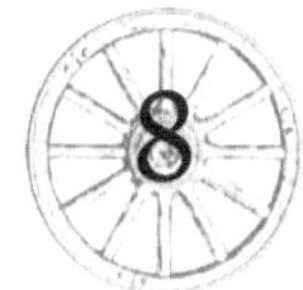

Why did she have to be so beautiful?

Sterling's chest ached as he watched Violet sleep. He knew he shouldn't be staring at her so openly and taking in every detail of her delicate features. But no one would have to know, since Hyacinth was still asleep and Violet was clearly tired too.

He'd checked the swelling in her ankle the last time he'd gotten up to add more wood to the stove, and it had been doing better. He'd been keeping an icy pack of snow on it off and on, and that had helped too.

With her body reclined and her head against the back of the chair, she'd managed to stay upright, although he'd repositioned her a time or two. He'd considered shifting his bench even closer so that she could lean against him if she wanted to. But that would be too much, wouldn't it?

Already, his following Violet out to Devil's Glen and the cabin bordered on crazy. Beckett had been sure to say so when Sterling had told his foreman of his plan to ski out to the cabin and see if the women were there.

He'd had to admit to Beckett the truth about the night before, how Violet and Hyacinth's father had betrayed them, how the women had stayed in the house, and then how they'd taken the food and the skis.

Of course, Beckett had been there for the wedding disaster back in April. The ranch foreman had witnessed firsthand all the pain and heartache Sterling had experienced on his wedding day and in the weeks afterward. So it only made sense that Beckett was leery about Violet now and didn't want Sterling to get involved in the situation.

But with the snowstorm, Sterling hadn't dared head out into the wilderness without informing his foreman where he was going. Because the truth was, he might not make it back to the ranch for a few days or maybe even longer.

He hadn't wanted to miss out on the vaccination of the cattle. He could very well return home to find the whole herd wiped out after Thatcher's administration of the vaccine. But they'd decided it was their only hope at this point, that if they didn't do something, they would lose all the cattle anyway.

Sterling just hoped he hadn't made a deadly mistake.

He tore his gaze from Violet and focused on the flames that were dancing inside the stove. During the trip up into Devil's Glen, he'd almost turned back a dozen times. She wasn't his responsibility anymore. He didn't love her or care about her or have an interest in what became of her.

Even though he'd berated himself during the difficult hike as he'd waded through the fresh snow and battled the wind, he'd kept going.

Now he was relieved he had. When he'd walked in on the women to discover they hadn't been able to start a fire, he'd almost cursed aloud. They might have made it through one night without heat, but they would have frozen to death eventually.

He blew out a breath.

"You should sleep too, Sterling." Violet's groggy whisper startled him.

He didn't move, though, from where he was leaning forward, resting his elbows on his knees. "How does your ankle feel?"

"It still hurts, but it's not quite as painful."

He nodded. Another sign that it wasn't broken and was only a sprain.

Silence settled back over the cabin, bringing with it the soft crackle of the wood burning in the stove. The wind had finally stopped its incessant noises, and a peaceful quiet had descended all around the cabin.

It was a beautiful place, but it was unforgivingly brutal too. Especially for two inexperienced women like

Violet and Hyacinth.

"Thank you for coming out here to help us," she said, as if reading his thoughts.

"I did what anyone else would have."

"You're not like everyone else." Her voice was not much more than a whisper.

What did she mean by that? It sounded like a compliment, like she even appreciated him. Irritation swelled just as swiftly as always when it came to his confusing feelings for her. "Let's be clear on one thing, Violet." He sat up and glared at her. "I didn't come out here because I still have feelings for you. I did it because I knew you two would die, and I didn't want to have a guilty conscience for the rest of my life."

Her eyes widened, making the lush green brighter and turning it into a place where he could lose himself. Except that he wasn't going to lose himself in her eyes ever again.

"I didn't expect you to have feelings for me still—"

"Then why did you come to me?" His question came out harsh, and the moment it did, he lowered his head and blew out a breath. "I'm sorry. I'm trying not to be angry. But it's hard."

She was silent for several heartbeats. "I should have gone to Hazel instead of you. She would have taken me and Hyacinth in. When we get back, I'll seek her out."

Hazel was like him and wouldn't turn away a person in need. "That would be for the best."

Violet dropped her gaze to her hands in her lap. "Okay."

He was being a donkey's hind end again. It was time to put the past behind him, wasn't it? He couldn't expect to move forward if he didn't stop being so angry with her all the time.

He swallowed his resentment and forced himself to speak calmly. "I went into town and talked to your father."

"You did?"

"I told him he had to figure a way out of his problems without involving you."

"And what did he say?" She seemed to be holding her breath.

"He said he would call off the deal, that it wasn't fair to you and Hyacinth to pressure you to work at the dancehall."

"Do you think he meant it?"

Sterling shrugged. "I hope so."

"I hope so too." Her voice didn't sound very confident.

"How long has he been gambling?" He knew he was prying, but didn't he deserve some answers?

"For a while." Her answer was quiet and resigned.

"Since your family moved to Breckenridge or before that?"

She hesitated, then sighed. "I cannot remember a time

in my life when he wasn't gambling."

The scope of her father's problems was much bigger and more longstanding than Sterling had expected. The same question he'd had earlier surfaced again. With something that had impacted her life so much, why hadn't she been honest about it? He'd courted her for months and had been about to marry her, and she'd never once hinted at the problem. "Why didn't you tell me?" The question fell out before he could stop it.

"It was—is—mortifying." Her face was pale except for her cheeks, which were splotchy with red—the sign she was embarrassed.

He shook his head. That wasn't reason enough. He opened his mouth to say so.

She spoke again before he could. "You always told me how perfect I was, and I didn't want to disappoint you."

What? He clamped his lips together.

She drew the blankets higher, as if in doing so she could protect herself from his wrath.

He *had* told her she was perfect. Because at the time, he'd believed she was, had thought that was a compliment. Had his declaration put too much pressure on her, perhaps even made her feel like she had to live up to his expectations?

Once again, a strange feeling pulsed through him— the feeling he bore much more responsibility in their relationship's demise than he'd realized.

"Besides, my mother always took care of the problems my father caused." Violet was staring straight ahead. "Once Mother was gone, Father had no one to clean up his messes anymore."

Mrs. Berkley had always seemed like a strong woman. "I'm sorry about your loss."

Violet nodded, her eyes turning glassy. "We didn't expect her to get so sick."

"What happened?"

For a little while, she shared about the past months living in Williamsburg, the city where her mother had grown up. As an only child whose father had owned a bank, Mrs. Berkley had inherited her parents' fortune when they'd passed away shortly after she'd turned eighteen. Not long after that, she'd married one of her father's bank tellers.

Although Mrs. Berkley's family had all been gone when she and her daughters had returned in the spring, she'd still had a few friends in Williamsburg and had been able to find a small apartment and some work taking in mending.

They'd been getting by well enough, hadn't been suffering, even if they'd had to live more simply and frugally than they ever had before. They'd made it through the summer, and then Mrs. Berkley had fallen ill with the influenza in September. She'd only lasted a month before dying.

"She made me promise to take care of Hyacinth," Violet whispered, her voice catching.

Sterling wanted to take Violet's hand in his and offer her some comfort. But he kept his hands clasped in front of him.

"I thought coming back to Colorado and living with our father would be best for us." She glanced over at her sister, who was curled up, the glow from the fire revealing a peaceful expression on her sleeping face. "But I only made things worse."

"You didn't know."

"I knew my father was a liar and couldn't be trusted." Her voice turned bitter. "His promises have always been empty."

"I didn't realize he was that way…He appeared so distinguished and respectable and responsible."

Violet released a soft but bitter laugh. "I didn't realize he was that way either until I was eight years old, on the day he sold my beloved mare Dixie, my very first horse, the pride and joy of my life."

Sterling's gut cinched with a new coil of anger. He'd already been mad at Mr. Berkley, and this only made his dislike even greater.

"We were moving. Again," Violet continued. "For about the hundredth time in my short life. When I begged Father not to sell Dixie, he said just as soon as we were settled into the new place, he'd send away for her."

"He never did?"

"Mother was the one to later tell me that he'd sold her to a slaughterhouse."

"Blast." Sterling wanted to release a string of curses to relieve the growing pressure in his chest. Instead, he stood to his feet and cracked his knuckles.

"Eventually Father apologized and promised me another horse of my own. But I never wanted another horse ever again."

Sterling wished he'd known all of this when he'd been courting Violet. Maybe it would have helped him understand her better, helped him be more sensitive to her needs. As it was, he could only stand rigidly, wishing he could pound his fist into Mr. Berkley's stomach.

"It's a good thing your father isn't here right now." He couldn't keep the contempt from his voice. "I'd be tempted to do him some damage."

Violet's lips curved into a ghost of a smile. "Thank you, Sterling. That's sweet of you."

What he wouldn't give to see one of her full smiles, one that made her pretty lips curl up high and brought a glow to her eyes. When was the last time he'd seen her smile? The truth was, she hadn't smiled a whole lot during those final few months leading up to the wedding. Maybe that should have alerted him that something wasn't right, that she wasn't happy.

But he'd been selfish, hadn't he? He'd only been

thinking about how happy being married to her would make *him*. He hadn't stopped to think about how *she* was feeling about everything.

"My father isn't all bad," she continued. "Deep down he does care about me and Hyacinth. I think that's what makes everything so much harder."

"That doesn't change my opinion of him."

Her smile inched higher.

His breath hitched. She was so beautiful when she smiled. And she was already way too beautiful when she was serious.

The familiar hollow ache in his chest pulsed a slow rhythm but wasn't as painful as it had been in the past when he'd thought about her and how much he'd loved her. Maybe this reunion—as hard as it had been so far—was a good thing and a way to bring about a resolution to all that had happened.

In talking with her and understanding her better, perhaps he'd be able to make peace with what had happened. He still might not like that she'd run away and rejected him, but he could accept that the situation had been more complex than he'd realized. And he needed to bear some of the blame too.

At the very least, he could bury the bitterness that had festered over the past months, couldn't he? Especially because it looked like they were going to be stuck together for a few days.

"Enough about my family." She waved a dismissive hand, as if that could somehow make her heartache and embarrassment go away. "Tell me about yours. Hazel is married and having a baby. What about everyone else?"

Her question was timid, as if she wasn't exactly sure how he would respond.

He lowered himself back to his bench. He would talk to her civilly, but that didn't mean he intended to be her friend again. No, the talking was just a way to pass the time. That's all it would be. Then when they returned to the ranch, they would go their separate ways and would never have to see each other again.

Violet's gaze kept straying to Sterling even though she was trying hard not to let it.

From her spot at the table with her half-finished supper in front of her, she was also having a difficult time eating the meal Hyacinth had prepared—canned beans and pork with canned peaches.

Sterling had already finished, pushed back from the table, and had resumed his whittling. He was positioned so that she had a good view of his profile—his muscular shoulder, angular jaw, and his hard mouth.

With his knife in hand, he shaved away at the wood in front of him, methodically and patiently, the curling woodchips falling to the floor at his boots.

Hyacinth had risen and was washing the dishes as best she could with the warm water on the stove. Her back was stiff, and every time she turned around, she glared at Sterling as if she wished the floorboards would open up and swallow him.

Violet had already scolded Hyacinth several times over the course of the long day about being nicer to Sterling. After all, if not for his coming after them, they would have been in a deadly predicament.

As it was, they'd slept as well as could be the previous night and had awoken to a warm cabin, the stove burning steadily with the fuel Sterling had added all throughout the night. It was obvious he'd rested very little, if at all, and at one point during the morning, Violet had encouraged him to get some sleep.

He'd finally flopped down on the opposite bunk bed without bothering to shed his boots and slumbered for a few hours. After waking up, he'd gone out to gather more wood, and in the process, he'd found some large pieces that he was now crafting into a sled. He hadn't needed to tell her why. She already knew he intended to use it to pull her back to the ranch, which would likely be the only way she'd be able to travel.

The few times she'd hobbled around on her sprained ankle, the pain had been too intense to stand for long. Sterling had indicated that her foot could take a few weeks to heal enough for her to walk on it. If that was the case, it would be much longer before she could manage to ski.

Sterling had explained that with the fresh layer of a foot or more of snow, even skiing would be challenging.

She guessed he could ski on it back to the ranch, that he was seasoned and experienced enough to do so. But he said he wanted to wait for some of it to melt before venturing out, probably so that he could pull the sled easier and also so that Hyacinth could manage her skis.

Whatever the case, Violet had resigned herself to a few days in the cabin with Sterling along with his silence and coldness. He'd surprised her earlier in the morning by listening without judgment to her explanation of her father's gambling problem. In fact, he hadn't thought less of her and had instead been angry at her father.

For whatever reason, that conversation had seemed to ease some of the tension between them so that they'd been able to talk a little more freely about how the past months had been for each of them and their families. He'd caught her up on where everyone in his family was—most of them out east, except that Jameson, one of his favorite brothers, had left home and they didn't know where he'd gone.

Their talking hadn't been as natural and easy as during the days when they'd been courting, but it had reminded her of how much she'd liked conversing with him.

She sensed he'd called a truce between them—at least while they were at the cabin. And she was willing to take whatever peace he was offering.

Unfortunately, Hyacinth didn't have the same mindset.

Violet pushed her plate back. "I've eaten all that I can."

Hyacinth shifted and took in the food still on Violet's plate. "No, you need to finish."

"You can have it. Or Sterling can." She knew for a fact that Sterling hadn't eaten his fill. He'd counted the cans earlier and taken inventory of what they had. She had no doubt he was rationing everything just in case they had to stay at the cabin longer.

Hyacinth fisted both hands on her hips. "You've hardly eaten all day, Vi."

"I agree," Sterling said without pausing in his repetitive whittling.

"I didn't ask for your opinion." Hyacinth's voice dripped with venom. "So I would appreciate you not adding it."

Sterling's back stiffened, and his knife on the wood came to an abrupt halt.

"Hyacinth," Violet scolded. "You're being rude."

She sniffed. "I don't care."

Sterling finally lifted his head and looked directly at Hyacinth. "Go ahead. Say it."

"Say what?"

"Whatever is bothering you."

With her green eyes flashing, Hyacinth pressed her lips together. She was loyal almost to a fault with the people she loved, and she'd somehow twisted the failed wedding around to make it Sterling's fault, blaming him for all that had happened.

"Hyacinth, please don't." Violet didn't want her sister dragging out the old hurts.

"Tell me, Hyacinth." Sterling's tone turned hard, as did his gaze. "What did I do to earn your contempt?"

Violet shook her head at her sister, silently pleading with her to let the matter drop.

Hyacinth sighed, then turned back around to the pot of soapy water on the stovetop.

Sterling didn't resume his whittling. Instead, he stood and propped the piece of wood against the cabin wall.

In the next instant, Hyacinth spun back around, her fingers dripping and her eyes blazing. "You're a selfish coward, Sterling."

He froze.

Violet grew motionless too. With the silence hanging thickly in the air, Violet had to say something. She shifted to face Sterling. "Hyacinth doesn't mean it—"

"I do mean it, Vi. You know how I feel. Sterling only thought of himself with the wedding and didn't consider your needs at all."

Violet's chest tightened. "Please, Hyacinth. Don't." She didn't want to lose the ground she'd made with Sterling—even as small as it was. Hyacinth spewing her feelings would not only cause a loss of ground; it would also erect a mountain between them.

Hyacinth, though, was focused on Sterling, had locked angry gazes with him. They were like two elk about to charge at each other. "What I don't understand, Sterling, is if you loved my sister the way you claimed, then why did you let her go without fighting for her?"

"I rode into town and tried to talk to Violet." Sterling's voice was calm but icy. "I even wrote to her. But she refused to see me or respond to my letters."

Hyacinth huffed. "A visit and letters? You call that fighting for her?"

"*She* ran away from our wedding. *She* said she didn't love me. *She* tossed me out of her life." Each statement was like a gunshot.

Violet hung her head. This was exactly what she hadn't wanted—for Sterling to hate her again.

"*She* was confused! If you'd really loved her, you would have been patient and understanding and tried to figure out what went wrong." Hyacinth's passionate declaration rang out in the cabin, echoing off the walls.

Violet waited tensely for Sterling to yell back, but this time he didn't say anything.

"If you'd really loved her," Hyacinth continued, "you wouldn't have let her leave Colorado and then never contacted her again. If you'd really loved her, you wouldn't have been able to live without her, and you would have gone after her."

Violet could feel her cheeks burning and the agony

twisting in her stomach. Hyacinth's tirade wasn't new to her. She'd heard her sister's frustration before. However, it was one thing to rant about Sterling in private and another to throw all the accusations in his face.

The pressure inside Violet pulsed up into her chest, urging her to get up and run outside and escape the embarrassment. She pushed back from the table, the need to flee only growing stronger with every passing second.

Before she could stand, Sterling muttered under his breath. Then he stalked across the room, swiped his coat from a peg on the wall, and without bothering to put it on, he swung the door wide and stepped outside.

As the door banged closed behind him, Violet lowered her head into her hands.

For long seconds, Violet could think of nothing but the fact that she'd lost Sterling again. The minuscule progress she'd made was gone.

That wasn't why she'd gone to him, was it? Because subconsciously she'd wanted to gain him back?

"I'm sorry, Vi." Hyacinth plopped down onto the end of the bench. "I don't know what came over me."

"Oh, Hyacinth. You shouldn't have—"

"Yes, I do know." Hyacinth slapped the table. "I'm just tired of him acting all hurt and angry at you. He needs to come off his high horse and stop treating you like you're the problem."

"But I am the problem."

"No!" Hyacinth reached over and grasped both of her hands. "You've always loved Sterling, and you still do."

"I don't know."

"Isn't that why we came back to Colorado?"

Was it? Violet hadn't thought so, but maybe, deep in her heart, she had wanted to see Sterling again and discover if he really did love her as much as he'd once claimed. "I've always been confused about my feelings toward Sterling. You know that."

"Maybe you're just afraid of Sterling ending up like our father."

Violet paused. Was her sister right? "In what way?"

"Father says he loves us but doesn't show it. When it comes down to it, he loves himself more than anyone."

Violet nodded. She hadn't thought about her father that way before, but Hyacinth's insights were true. Father had always lived the way he wanted regardless of the consequences for their family. Every place they'd moved to, he'd promised Mother he would do better, that he would keep his job, that he would stay away from the gaming tables.

Yet at every new place, he'd eventually ended up gambling again, stealing from his employer to pay his debt, getting fired, and then needing Mother to come to his rescue before they moved, and the cycle started all over again.

Mother had paid off Father's debts so often over the

years that she'd used up her sizable inheritance getting him out of trouble, leaving them with too little in the end.

Was that why Father had married Mother to begin with? Because he'd known she would take care of him?

Violet wanted to think he'd loved Mother to some degree, the same way she wanted to believe he loved her and Hyacinth. But what if he'd never really been able to love anyone but himself?

Hyacinth squeezed Violet's hands. "Maybe you just need to know Sterling is different from Father. Maybe then you'll finally be able to give yourself permission to love him with your whole heart instead of holding back."

Violet lifted her head and met her sister's gaze. "But is Sterling different? Is any man?"

Hyacinth's eyes were filled with sadness. "I hope so, Vi. I really hope so. But I don't know."

Sterling stomped a path in the snow in front of the cabin, frustration pounding through his blood, and Hyacinth's words about Violet ringing in his head.

If you'd really loved her, you would have been patient and understanding and tried to figure out what went wrong.

If you'd really loved her, you wouldn't have let her leave Colorado and then never contacted her again.

If you'd really loved her, you wouldn't have been able to live without her, and you would have gone after her.

Was Hyacinth right on every count? Was he a selfish coward?

The light coming from the window illuminated the small cleared area in front of the cabin and the pine trees that surrounded it, still heavy with snow.

He paused his pacing and peered up at the sky, which was clear and studded with a million stars. The stillness and quietness of the winter night usually brought him a measure of peace. But tonight, turmoil roiled inside him.

For so many months, he'd felt justified in his anger and resentment toward Violet and hadn't stopped to consider the situation from any other perspective.

What if he'd been wrong about everything? What if he'd even been wrong about love?

He'd never made time for women in his life before he'd met Violet. He'd been too busy on the ranch, too busy trying to prove to his dad that he could run it and make it successful.

Of course, he'd always planned to get married. In fact, he and Maverick had even told each other where they wanted to propose to the women they loved. He'd thought he'd fallen in love with Violet, had never felt so strongly for any other woman, had loved everything about her.

But what if his love for Violet had been selfish and more about what *she* could do for him and add to his life than what *he* could do for her? Hyacinth was right that he hadn't been patient or understanding with Violet. He hadn't considered her needs and how she'd been feeling on their wedding day—or when he'd proposed and she'd initially rejected him.

No, he'd only been thinking about himself, how she'd wronged him and how she'd pushed him away.

If he'd really loved her—unconditionally and unselfishly—maybe he would have had a different perspective on all that had happened. Maybe he would have reacted more maturely. Maybe he wouldn't have held on to his bitterness for so long.

His shoulders slumped, and he dropped his head. He'd been a fool, that's what. A stubborn fool. It was past time to forgive Violet and seek her forgiveness for all that had happened. That was the first place to start in making amends.

The second way to make amends was to assist her through this whole situation with her father and his debt. Violet desperately needed a friend who would be there for her and keep her safe from whatever plans her father had made with Claude.

Sterling pinned his gaze on the cabin door. He didn't still love her and couldn't imagine ever resuming a relationship with her. But he could be the help she so badly needed, couldn't he? Without expecting anything in return?

Then someday, when he'd worked on himself and learned more about what it meant to love sacrificially, maybe he'd be ready to meet someone new—someone he could love the right way this time.

Steeling his shoulders, he started back to the door. No more excuses. He had to let go of the past and move on. As he reached the door, he hesitated only a moment before swinging it wide and stepping inside.

The two women were at the table where he'd left

them, and their gazes swung to him and their conversation came to an abrupt halt. Obviously they'd been talking about him. No doubt Hyacinth was telling Violet all the things that were wrong with him. And no doubt she would be right about most of them.

He closed the door, then stood in front of it, not sure what to do next. He took off his hat, slicked back his hair, then slapped his hat back on while expelling a tight breath.

Both women sat quietly and watched him with rounded eyes. Hyacinth's expression was no longer filled with hostility and instead held sadness. Violet also seemed resigned, as if she'd accepted the end of their relationship as they'd once known it.

"Listen, Violet." He cracked his knuckles, then stuffed his hands into his pockets. "Hyacinth was right about everything. I was selfish and cowardly, and I only thought of myself instead of thinking of what was best for you."

"I did the same," Violet responded softly.

"You already apologized," he said just as softly. "Now it's my turn."

She crossed her hands on the table in front of her. "As you said, I ran away from our wedding. I told you I didn't love you. I tossed you out of my life."

Yes, she'd done all that. But that was no excuse for letting so much hate embitter him, especially because he'd lost track of the fact that he wasn't perfect either and had problems that had affected them too.

"If I'd really loved you, I would have cared about how you were feeling and would have taken the time to listen and understand instead of rushing you into something you weren't ready for."

"Oh, wow," Violet whispered, tears turning her eyes glossy.

She obviously hadn't expected him to confess his shortcomings. Why had it taken him so long to do so?

Hyacinth stood and stretched with a loud yawn. "I'm tired and going to bed." She bent and placed a kiss on Violet's head.

"Good night." Violet gave her sister a wobbly smile.

Hyacinth cupped Violet's cheek, stared at her for a long second—as though imparting strength—then turned and walked toward one of the bunk beds.

He sensed Hyacinth was doing her best to allow him and Violet some privacy, although she would still be able to hear every word of their conversation in the one-room cabin.

Even so, he appreciated her willingness to let them talk alone. She clearly cared enough for Violet that she wanted her sister to find some resolution in all that had happened.

A few moments later, when Hyacinth was motionless beneath her covers, Sterling cleared his throat and started his apology again. "I'm sorry for being selfish. I realize now that I entered our relationship looking at all the ways you could meet my needs, fit into my life, and make me happy."

The words came more easily than he'd expected, maybe because on some level he'd already known he'd been selfish. Whatever the case, he needed to do this, not just for her but for himself, so that he could find healing and release. Ignoring the problem and trying to forget about Violet hadn't helped him. The bitterness had only festered and spread.

In real life, true healing never came from overlooking the physical wound. It came from doing the painful work of cleaning and treating and bandaging it. The same was clearly true of emotional wounds.

"I thought I knew what love was," he continued. "But I realize now that I have a lot to learn."

"Don't be too hard on yourself, Sterling." She'd cocked her head and was studying him, as if seeing him for the first time.

Maybe this was a first—a first in the many lessons he still needed to learn, this one about humility. After all, he had a hard time being humble, admitting he was wrong, and giving up his grudges. He only had to think about how he'd almost ruined his relationship with Maverick and Hazel earlier in the year to be reminded just how stubborn he was.

"You're a good man," Violet said sincerely, "and you

were good to me."

"Does that mean you forgive me?"

"There's nothing to forgive—"

"I could have done things differently too. Much differently."

"That's kind of you to say." She lowered her gaze to the table, which was a good thing because he never had been able to resist the pretty green of her eyes. "But I'm realizing that with my father the way he is, I probably have a difficult time trusting in love. He always claimed to love me, said he loved me. But if he really did, how could he give me and Hyacinth up so easily?"

Sterling hadn't thought of the connection, but he supposed that made sense. What good did a profession of love serve if it wasn't backed up with actions? Had he done the same thing to Violet—made declarations of love but then given her up?

"I'm sorry I was like your father." After learning the truth about Mr. Berkley, he didn't want to be anything like the fellow. "But I'm learning, and I hope to become a man who loves with actions first and words second."

A small smile played upon her lips.

The stiffness in his muscles eased. "I'll be a better man someday...and my future wife will have you to thank for it."

Her smile faded. "Of course."

He probably hadn't needed to mention his future

wife. But he didn't want Violet to think he had plans to become a better man for *her*. Just because they'd apologized to each other and begun to make peace didn't mean he had any intention of pursuing her again.

Once had been enough.

"So, will you tell me more about Maverick and Hazel?" she asked shyly, clearly changing the subject. "I'd love to hear how they got together."

"It's a long story."

"I've got nowhere else to go." She waved a hand at the room to make her point.

He hesitated.

Her smile dimmed even more, disappearing altogether. "You don't have to—"

"I've got nowhere else to go either." He tried to lighten his voice. Talking to her hadn't hurt him last night, and it wouldn't hurt anything tonight either. In fact, he was looking forward to sitting in the quiet of the cabin again and conversing with her. Just like old acquaintances who were catching up with each other. That was all.

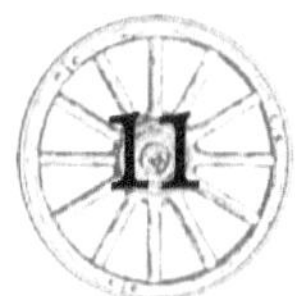

Pinecones, spruce, and holly berries.

Violet stood back from the table and eyed the cabin, smiling at the transformation she'd brought to it during the past day of decorating.

"It does look a little Christmassy." The pinecones and boughs around the door were especially pretty with the light-brown calico ribbon Hyacinth had sewn. The spruce wreath on the wall above the table was stunning too, with the larger pinecones Sterling had collected for her. The table centerpiece complemented everything with shorter spruce limbs and a few sprigs of holly berry arranged in a glass jar.

Sitting on the bench at the table, Hyacinth was hemming a placemat out of the calico material from an old skirt that had grown too frayed to use anymore, and Violet planned to put the placemat underneath the glass jar at the center of the table.

"Maybe I shouldn't use the holly berries." Violet leaned against the crutch Sterling had crafted for her out of a stick, keeping the pressure off her sprained ankle.

Sterling had wanted her to sit again today, like she had all day yesterday, and keep her foot elevated. But she'd been too restless and had needed to do something to occupy her time.

Since decorating was one of her passions, she'd decided to liven up the cabin interior as best she could. Sterling had insisted on being the one to collect all the supplies she'd required, directing her back to the chair every time he came inside and saw she was standing.

In between collecting her decorations, he'd made progress on the sled and was nearly finished. He'd also been keeping an eye on the weather. The sun had been out all day and melted some of the new snow, so he was hoping they could travel back to the ranch safely tomorrow.

With Sterling there helping them and keeping them safe, a part of her didn't want to leave. They were far away from Father and Claude and all that had gone wrong, and she liked not having to worry about those problems. It was easier avoiding the issues rather than addressing them. Maybe that had been her approach with Sterling and their relationship back in the spring too, and look how that had worked out.

Regardless of when they were leaving the cabin, the

decorating project had been an enjoyable way to spend the day, which had been mostly peaceful. Some tension still existed, although it wasn't as bad since the conversation last night and Sterling's apology.

Violet had gone to bed shortly after their discussion, sleeping again with Hyacinth while Sterling took the bottom bunk across from them. With him so close by, she'd slept restlessly, thinking about his apology off and on all night. He'd been very sweet to take Hyacinth's rebuke to heart and to express his shortcomings. He'd even listened to her talk about her difficulty in trusting men as it related to her father, and he'd seemed to understand and had even apologized for being like her father.

Even so, he'd been clear at the end of their conversation that he wasn't interested in her any longer and that he planned to choose a different wife someday. Although she'd been discouraged by his statement, she wasn't surprised that he didn't want her. Because, despite his apology, she still didn't blame Sterling for anything that had gone wrong. In fact, the more she considered her father and his issues, the more she realized how that had influenced her view of Sterling and other men.

As much as she wanted to believe she could heal and change, she would always have the scars. Ultimately, Sterling would be better off with another woman—one who was stronger and more stable.

The door opened, and Sterling stepped inside, filling the cottage with his presence. With his broad shoulders, heavy coat, and towering frame, he seemed to take up all the space. Maybe it was his brawny physique, or maybe it was the commanding air about him that made him so powerful. Whatever it was, every time he came in, she found herself having to take a step back, as if in doing so she could put some space between them.

He was carrying a tin pail, and it was heaped full of more pinecones.

She started to hobble toward him. "Oh, wonderful! You found enough for a garland."

His eyes narrowed on her. "How long have you been standing?"

"Only a few minutes."

He nodded at the chair she'd abandoned. "Sit."

She wasn't a defiant person and mostly complied to whatever the situation required, so she hesitated only a moment before using her crutch to limp back to her spot.

Truthfully, she liked that Sterling was concerned about her. His concern was better than the aloof attitude he'd displayed when he'd discovered her on his porch. His doting reminded her of how he'd always showered her with such kindness and respect when they'd been courting. It was one of the many qualities she'd liked about him. He'd treated his mother and sisters the same way, deferring to them, assisting them, and looking out for their well-being.

Violet had never had brothers to watch over her, and Father had rarely shown that kind of consideration. There was only one time in her life she remembered fondly—a short few weeks when they'd lived in Missouri when she'd been twelve. Father had arrived home every evening after work, they'd eaten dinner as a family, and he'd read stories afterward. Some evenings, he'd taken walks with her and Hyacinth, and one time they'd stopped at a park and fed the ducks.

She'd wanted those evenings with Father to last forever. For the first time, she'd felt like they were a real family and that he truly loved her.

But the time with him had ended all too soon, and Father had been busy again. At that time, she hadn't realized what monopolized his life. Now she knew that he'd been gambling, that his draw to the cards and poker table had been stronger than his draw to his family.

She'd always wondered what had changed during those few weeks of normalcy. Had he tried to quit? Had he wanted to do better but never had the strength to follow through? It was almost as if he was addicted to gambling—if that were even possible.

She sat down and propped her foot on the second chair.

Only then did Sterling shrug out of his coat. He tossed it on one of the hooks, then headed toward the stove. "Is the molasses and sugar boiling?"

"Yes." Hyacinth expelled an exasperated breath. "I stirred it as you requested."

Sterling reached the stove and peered into the pot where he'd poured all their molasses as well as quite a bit of their sugar. He hadn't said what he was doing, only that he wanted to make something for them.

Hyacinth hadn't been excited and was irritated at Sterling again, having admitted earlier today that she hadn't liked Sterling's *future wife* comment from last evening. She thought that, once again, Sterling was being a coward and not fighting for his relationship with Violet.

Violet hadn't admitted to her sister that the comment had stung a little. Instead, she'd insisted that Sterling had every right to choose someone else since she'd already had her chance and had thrown it away. Even if a secret part of her had hoped Sterling might still care about her, she also respected that he wanted to move on to a different woman and didn't want to be burdened by her problems and issues.

Sterling swirled a wooden spoon in the mixture, then stood back and glanced her way. "Are you ready to make snow candy?"

"Snow candy?" Violet sat up. "What's that?"

"I'll show you." Sterling returned to the door, stepped outside for a few moments, then came back carrying two plates filled with perfectly white powdery snow.

He placed one plate in front of Violet and the other near Hyacinth, who set down her sewing and eyed the snow warily.

Sterling lifted the pan with the molasses–sugar mixture to the table. He dipped the spoon into the pan, scooped up a spoonful, then dribbled the golden mixture into the snow, twirling it to make a circle. When finished, he gingerly picked up the now-solid molasses.

"Snow candy." He held out the piece.

She studied the glassy circle-shaped candy. "It looks interesting."

"Try it."

She hesitated.

He broke off a piece and touched it to her mouth.

Was he actually feeding her candy?

She raised her gaze to his to find that his eyes were nearly the same color as the candy—a sugary light brown. They were warm with kindness and tenderness and nothing more.

Did she want his eyes to hold attraction—the desire that had flared on occasion when they'd been courting?

Maybe she did. Maybe she wanted to try again with him, even though everything in her told her she shouldn't, that she needed to let him go. Wasn't that what she'd been telling herself all day? Even just moments ago?

She'd never been good at flirting, had never interacted

much with men before meeting Sterling. She supposed that whenever her family had moved, she'd been hesitant to form relationships with men much the same way she'd been hesitant to form friendships with women, because she was embarrassed about her family's problems and had wanted to keep them a secret.

But now Sterling knew all her secrets. He even knew how low her father had fallen to be willing to send her and Hyacinth to be dancehall girls.

She had nothing to lose with Sterling, did she? Could she take a chance and see if he might learn to like her again?

Without breaking her gaze from his, she parted her lips.

His attention dropped to her mouth, and he slipped the candy inside.

As the sugary treat touched her tongue, she closed her mouth to savor the grainy sweetness, and her lips made contact with two of his fingers.

He froze with his eyes locked on her mouth.

She grew motionless too. A part of her knew she needed to open her mouth and pull back. But this contact with his fingers was somehow exciting, the touch of him reminding her of the few times they'd kissed and how his lips had felt against hers—so soft and tender and also heated and filled with desire.

As if hearing her thoughts, or perhaps remembering

their kisses too, his gaze slid back up to hers. This time the brown was a rich molasses, thick and dark. He held her gaze as though he couldn't make himself let go, as though he wanted the moment to last, as though maybe, just maybe, he did still feel something for her.

Her heart fluttered with something of her own.

In the next instant, though, he swallowed hard, his Adam's apple prominent in his throat. He dropped his hand from her mouth, glanced away, and took a step back, palming the back of his neck and looking everywhere but at her.

She closed her mouth over the candy and tried to focus on the deliciousness, but her mind was still processing the taste of Sterling and the pleasure of the contact with him.

Clearing his throat, Sterling reached for the spoon in the pan and filled it with more of the molasses liquid. "We have to make the candy before the snow melts." He dribbled another spoonful onto Violet's plate.

Hyacinth's gaze was bouncing between Violet and Sterling, one brow quirked. When Sterling finished making another piece of candy, he handed the spoon to Hyacinth, and she began making her own formations in the snow.

As the piece in Violet's mouth dissolved, she reached for the second piece of candy Sterling had created.

"Did you like it?" Sterling asked. Was there a hopeful note to his voice?

Her heart gave another soft flutter. She knew she shouldn't let herself feel anything for Sterling. She didn't want to hurt him again. And she didn't want to put herself into a position where she might be hurt too.

Even so, she couldn't keep from smiling up at him. "I loved it."

His lips turned up into a grin—one that made the corners of his eyes crinkle with genuine pleasure.

Oh, she'd missed his grins. And yes, maybe it was finally time to admit how much she'd missed him and to acknowledge to herself that was why she'd come back to Colorado—because a big part of her heart belonged to him and maybe always would.

"Thank you for this, Sterling." She waved a hand at the snow candy and at the pinecones. "I haven't had this much fun in a long time."

Hyacinth snorted.

Violet tossed her sister a censuring sideways look. "It *is* fun." Hyacinth had never enjoyed decorating as much as Violet and their mother. She'd always done so grudgingly and only if it involved sewing, which was something she loved doing.

Hyacinth paused with a piece of candy halfway to her mouth and pinned a narrowed look on Sterling. "This whole experience is not fun. Not when I have to worry about Sterling's motivation for being nice all of a sudden."

"Hyacinth." Violet couldn't keep from scolding her sister. "We're just trying to put the past behind us, and maybe it's time for you to do the same."

"I don't trust you, Sterling." Hyacinth didn't take her gaze from him. "You hurt Violet once. How can I be assured you aren't going to hurt her again?"

"Stop, Hyacinth." Embarrassment surged through Violet, and she pushed up from the table, heedless of her ankle. "Sterling has always been a nice man to everyone. And that's all this is. Nothing more."

Sterling didn't say anything. Instead, his eyes were locked with Hyacinth's in a hard, silent battle of wills.

"Just tell me you'll do better this time," Hyacinth said evenly.

Violet released an exasperated sigh. What was Hyacinth talking about? "There is no *this time*."

"We'll see about that." Hyacinth quirked one brow, then popped the piece of molasses candy into her mouth, all the while holding the stare with Sterling.

Sterling was finally the one to turn away, his back straight, his shoulders rigid.

Violet frowned and mouthed the word *stop* to her sister.

Hyacinth shrugged nonchalantly and took another bite of the candy.

Blowing out a long breath, Sterling reached for the sled he'd been fashioning, lowered himself to one of the chairs, and began working on it. No doubt he was thinking that the sooner he finished, the sooner he would be able to return home. Because no matter how nice he might be, their time together didn't mean anything, and Violet couldn't start to believe that it did.

From where she lay in the bunk, Violet couldn't keep from watching Sterling as he locked the cabin door for the night. She and Hyacinth left the lantern on the table lit for him so that he didn't have to walk inside to complete darkness.

He'd gone out for a little bit, telling them he wanted to check around the cabin and make sure everything looked all right. But Violet knew that he'd also stepped outside to allow her and Hyacinth to get ready for bed.

He was always so considerate.

Even now as he slipped off his boots, he did so quietly, likely not wanting to disturb them. He hung his coat on the peg next to the door, then turned and scanned the room, his gaze landing on the lower bunk bed where she was lying next to Hyacinth. Her sister had fallen asleep easily, clearly able to put all their concerns out of her mind—something Violet wasn't as good at doing.

What was he thinking now after the past couple of days? He wasn't exactly warm toward her, but the anger and disdain and even the coldness had dissipated. He hadn't needed to make the snow candy earlier, but for some reason, he had.

"How is your ankle?" he whispered.

She wiggled her toes and felt only a small twinge of pain. The swelling had gone down, and the pain had diminished, likely because of his vigilance in keeping her ankle iced and elevated as well as preventing her from walking around. "It's getting better, thanks to you and your doctoring."

"Good."

She tugged her blanket up.

He frowned. "Are you cold?" Before she could answer, he crossed to the stove and began to add more wood to the flames.

When he straightened, he stared at the fire for a few seconds before shifting to look at her again. "Hopefully that keeps you warm for a while."

"You're such a kind man, Sterling." She was growing warmer, but not from the stove's heat. It was from his scrutiny, the way he seemed to linger over her. And yes, it was also because she was letting herself get her fill of him. In the dim lighting, his features were even more chiseled, his jaw strong, his cheekbones prominent, and his scruff dark. He was all brawn, lean and muscular.

She hadn't met many cowboys before Sterling, and she'd been fascinated by him from the moment he'd introduced himself to her. Tonight, at this moment, as her gaze slid down him, she couldn't keep from noticing just how incredibly appealing his body was—a body that had been honed and shaped by the land and weather and the animals he raised.

The warmth inside seeped deeper, creating a strange craving to be close to him, to lie next to him and press against that hard chest.

What in heaven's name was she thinking?

She quickly shifted her gaze to her blanket. Why was she having such wanton thoughts? She'd never had brazen desires for him previously. So why now?

Was it because of their close living quarters? Because she was in bed and sleeping so near to him? Or because he was more rugged and handsome and attractive than she'd remembered?

For several moments, she could hear him shuffling around the cabin. She kept her gaze off him, half afraid to look at him again in case she stirred up more cravings for him.

Besides, she didn't want him to see it. That would be mortifying.

Finally, he put out the light, then made his way in the darkness to the bunk bed across from her and situated himself there.

When all was silent again, she allowed herself to take a peek at him. She'd expected to have to strain to see him in the darkness, but the glow from the fire provided enough light that she could see he was lying on his side, facing her, his eyes closed. With the frustration and determination gone from his face, he was even better looking—so much so that her heart pattered an extra-hard beat.

She situated herself more comfortably on her side. Maybe she would watch him all night. Would that be odd? Too much?

She let her gaze linger on the arm that he'd tucked under his head to act as a pillow. His shirt was taut against his bicep, his hair thick and mussed, and his shoulders relaxed.

He cracked open an eye and raised one brow at her as though questioning her scrutiny.

Oh bother. How had he known she was staring? She prayed that, through the darkness, he couldn't see how mortified she was that he'd caught her ogling him.

"I'm sorry for sending you away." His whisper was unexpected, as was his apology, and the sincerity in his eyes was almost more than she knew what to do with. "I shouldn't have told you to leave the house by dawn."

"It's all right. I understand why—"

"No, I was wrong and rude and insensitive."

"Sterling..." A powerful affection swelled inside

her—an affection that was unlike anything she'd felt before. Once again, she wanted to be close to him and let him wrap her in his arms all night long. Instead, she closed her eyes to hide that longing from him and herself.

"Good night, Violet." His voice was a caress.

"Good night," she whispered, fighting the urge to open her eyes. If she did, she wasn't sure what she might do with all the strange yearnings that were pulsing through her with growing intensity. The best thing was for her to go to sleep and force herself to forget that Sterling was there.

In fact, the best thing was to forget that she was attracted to him at all.

Sterling's muscles burned from the exertion of pulling Violet on the sled. But the ranch was in sight, and he'd kept the two women safe for the duration of the long hike down from the miner's cabin.

Although they'd left early in the morning, it was already past midday. The journey had taken twice as long as it usually did, not just because the sled had slowed them down but because the snow had been thick and treacherous in some places. He'd had to circle off the trail so that the way would be smoother. A few times he'd even lifted Violet onto his back and carried her through areas that had been too rough for the sled.

Relief and gratefulness welled inside him that they'd made it back. He hadn't wanted to cause Violet more pain during the journey, but he also hadn't wanted to chance staying and having another storm blow in, trapping them even longer. Not when the amount of food had already been slim.

He paused on the final rise and took in the sight. Nestled in the valley, the ranch was picturesque, with the rugged mountain range in the east rising up and dwarfing the house and the barns and the outbuildings. Everything looked so peaceful with the fresh snow covering the pastures, and the cattle milling about in the field also appeared to be fine.

Were they, though? How many more steers had died while he'd been gone? The closer he'd gotten to home, the more he'd begun to dread what he'd find.

Behind him, he could feel Violet wiggling out of the sled.

He glanced over his shoulder at her. "Hold on now."

But he was too late. She was already climbing to her feet and using her crutch to propel herself upward. "I want to see the view too." She was bundled in layers of clothing and her coat and hood and mittens. But none of the heavy garments could hide just how beautiful she was, especially with her cheeks flushed, wisps of dark hair loose from her braid, and the green of her eyes so bright in the sunshine.

Hyacinth, who had followed behind the sled, halted beside Violet and steadied her.

The snow on the precipice was thinner, almost melted in some places. At least the rocky terrain was easy to cross as Violet hobbled forward.

She'd been there several times with him in the past. They'd even shared a kiss one time while standing and overlooking the ranch. He'd been brimming with such excitement at that time, holding her in his arms and thinking he had his future secured—a soon-to-be wife and the start of his own family, and the ranch that his dad said would be Sterling's someday. He'd believed he had everything he needed.

But once again the plans had been about him. He hadn't stopped to consider what Violet might want. He'd been too focused on how she was making his life better and fulfilling his dreams.

Her crutch slipped in the snow, causing her to wobble. Even though Hyacinth still had a hold of her, Sterling slid toward Violet and latched onto her other arm. "I'll carry you."

She hesitated.

"I'll have to help you down the last hill. It's too steep for the sled." The sled, while rudimentary, had done the job of getting her out of the mountains. He had his brother Jameson to thank for having some carpentry skills. His younger brother, the middle child of their family, had a knack for building things and had always had a special place in Sterling's heart, probably because the two of them hadn't gone to college the way their dad had wanted.

But Jameson had taken off midway through the

summer after a heated argument with their dad. Sterling hadn't been present during the argument that morning. Apparently it had been like so many of the others, with Dad telling Jameson he needed to stop riding into town and spending so much time at the saloons, except at the end, Dad had issued an ultimatum and told Jameson to stop all the carousing or find a new place to live and work.

The next morning, Jameson had packed his bag and ridden away. They hadn't heard from him since. They had no idea where he'd gone or even if he was still alive.

All Sterling had left were memories of his brother, and he'd thought of Jameson a lot while creating the sled. He'd appreciated that, during their stay at the cabin, Violet had asked about his family and specifically Jameson, that she'd remembered Sterling's connection with his brother. He'd also appreciated how well she'd listened to him as he'd shared his worries and grief that Jameson was gone. Violet had always been a good listener and still was.

"Climb up." He cocked his head toward his back.

She sighed and reached for his shoulder. "You've already carried me enough."

"I don't mind." Truth be told, he'd relished the few times he'd already had her on his back. He'd liked having her close and feeling the pressure of her body against his.

As she began to hoist herself up, he bent and helped

to situate her. She tossed her crutch onto the sled with their valises, and then he started forward again with her legs wrapped around his torso and her arms snaked around his neck. She was lithe and light, but under her weight, he sank lower into the snow and had to work harder to propel his skis.

"I haven't had the chance to thank you yet, Sterling." Her voice rumbled behind his ear, and in the next instant, he could feel her warm breath against his neck. She was closer than the previous times he'd carried her. Or maybe she was just leaning in so she could talk to him and didn't realize how intimate the movement felt.

Maybe it wasn't intimate, and he only thought it was because he couldn't get the image of her lips around his fingers from his mind. He hadn't meant to create a charged moment with her last evening, but what had he expected after putting a piece of the snow candy into her mouth? Anything that had to do with her pretty lips was sure to make him think all kinds of thoughts about what it would be like to kiss her again.

As usual, Hyacinth had noticed, had easily seen through all the walls he'd tried to erect to keep Violet out and prevent himself from letting her in. Hyacinth had seen something in him—maybe the long-buried feelings for Violet—and had warned him to do better this time.

He'd almost protested, but Violet had beaten him to it. He agreed. There wouldn't be a *this time*. But he respected Hyacinth for loving Violet so much and pushing him to be careful.

"So thank you for coming after us." Violet's words seemed to caress his neck. "We wouldn't have made it if not for you."

"I only did what anyone else would have."

"No, you didn't." Her arms tightened around his neck as she leaned in even closer. "Most people wouldn't have taken the risk in going out to the cabin, especially for someone they didn't like."

Was she right? Sterling couldn't imagine just sitting back during the storm and leaving the two women to fend for themselves, even if he didn't like them. Which wasn't the case anymore. Maybe it had never been the case.

"I don't dislike you, Violet." He could at least make that clear.

"You'd rather not be near me, though."

He was finding her nearness at the moment thoroughly enjoyable, but he couldn't say that. "We're fine now. We forgave each other, and we're moving on. Right?"

"Right."

As he approached the trailhead at the edge of the precipice, he glanced over his shoulder to see how Hyacinth was doing. Instead, he found his face mere inches from Violet's, close enough that she could press a kiss to his cheek.

But he didn't want her kissing his cheek or breathing on his neck. He didn't want to raise to life the attraction that needed to remain dead. That desire had already tried to resurrect itself, and he kept having to shove it back into the casket.

He shifted his focus back to the trail ahead and the difficult navigation, sidestepping carefully down through the rocks.

She expelled another breath that was warm and much too distracting. "When we get back to your ranch, I'll send Hyacinth over to High C Ranch to talk to Hazel about staying with her."

Staying with Hazel probably would be for the best.

Even though he'd vowed he would make amends to Violet and help her out of the situation with her father, he couldn't have her stay at his ranch with him, could he? Her presence there would cause all kinds of pesky gossip and rumors. And after the failed wedding, he'd already been the center of conversations enough for one year.

"I'll see if Alonzo is available to drive Hyacinth over."

"I'm sure she would like that." Violet's arms loosened just slightly from around his neck, or maybe he was imagining it.

She was quiet the rest of the way down the hill, which was for the best so that he could concentrate on not falling. When they reached level ground again, he went back for the sled. At his return, he helped situate her back on it with the bags wedging her in. Then they began crossing the last field that separated the ranch from the foothills.

As they drew closer to the house, one of the ranch hands spotted them and called out. A minute later, Beckett was on his horse and riding toward them. As he drew up, something in the young man's face set Sterling on edge.

Had the vaccine started killing off the cattle in addition to the blackleg? How many more livestock had died in the few days he'd been gone?

"What's wrong?" He halted and tipped up the brim of his Stetson.

Beckett twisted a piece of hay between his teeth, as he usually did. He took in both Violet and Hyacinth before settling his gaze on Sterling. "Glad you made it there, boss. Was worried."

The conditions hadn't been great when Sterling had set out for the cabin, and he was sorry for having worried his friend. But he'd had little choice. "Violet hurt her ankle. Otherwise we're none the worse for wear."

"Good." Beckett's attention drifted again to the women, first to Violet then to Hyacinth, where his gaze stayed for a few seconds too long.

"How are things here?" Sterling almost didn't want to ask the question, and he braced himself for the answer.

"For the cattle?" Beckett nodded toward the field closest to the barns, where the steers were mostly clustered around mounds of hay from among the fodder they grew and stored for the winter months, when snow made grazing difficult. "Only one more died after you left."

The tension inside Sterling snapped loose, and he almost sagged in relief. "Then the vaccine is working?"

Beckett gave a curt nod. "Thatcher has over half the herd vaccinated, and so far they're all doing just fine."

"No signs of problems in them?"

"Not a one. We owe Thatcher a huge debt. He's been here every day from dawn to well past dusk doling out the shots."

"That's mighty nice of him."

"He's a good veterinarian and a real good man." Beckett's voice, with his thick Southern drawl, trailed off as though he had more to say—news he didn't want to speak around the women. Something else was wrong.

Sterling's muscles tensed.

Behind him, Violet sniffled, then sneezed.

He propelled himself forward again. "Let's get the women inside. Then we can talk some more."

Beckett shifted his horse around so that he was plodding alongside Sterling. "Not sure if you should take the women to the house, boss."

"Why not?"

Beckett leaned in and dropped his voice. "The house

was ransacked two nights ago."

"What?" Sterling stumbled over his skis and nearly fell. As he straightened, he stopped and glanced around with a new sense of alertness, this time taking in the distant snowy fields they used for alfalfa, the split-rail fences, the two grain silos, the barns and bunkhouse and storage sheds. The large house stood a short distance apart, showcasing his family's status and wealth. Everything seemed in order as it should be.

"Someone broke into the house." Beckett spoke a little louder.

"I heard you the first time." Sterling glared at the man and then nodded at the women.

But it was too late. Violet's eyes had widened at the news, and her lashes seemed darker than usual as they framed her eyes.

"Did you see who did it?" Sterling asked.

Beckett shook his head. "Must have happened when we were out with the herd, because we didn't see anyone."

"Alonzo notice anything?"

"He heard some noise while he was rustling up grub and went out to investigate and saw a couple fellows leaving the house."

Sterling's jaw tightened with the need to curse.

Beckett nodded solemnly. "Men said they worked for Claude St. Germaine from the Red Cap Saloon and were looking for two women."

Violet began pushing up from the sled, her expression worried. "They wanted us."

"Reckon so." Beckett's gaze bounced to Hyacinth again as she helped Violet up.

Why had Claude sent his men to look for Violet and Hyacinth at the ranch? Maybe Mr. Berkley had told Claude about Sterling's visit to the house and his concern for the women. Maybe Claude had heard about Sterling's previous engagement to Violet and had concluded he might shelter the sisters.

Of course, Claude would be right. Sterling had been protecting them.

Violet straightened herself, favoring her uninjured foot. "I'm sorry for bringing the danger to the ranch, Sterling. We will leave right away."

"And go where?" He couldn't keep the frustration from his voice. "You can't go to High C Ranch and chance bringing the danger to Hazel." He wouldn't put his sister in that kind of predicament ever, but especially not when she was expecting a baby.

Violet pursed her lips and shifted to look at the foothills they'd just hiked out of. Was she thinking of returning to the cabin?

He shook his head, a strange sense of desperation starting to gnaw at him. "No, don't even think about it. I won't let you go back out there with Hyacinth alone. Not without me or someone else who can keep you safe."

"We'll be fine—"

"What if Claude's men hear about the cabin and decide to trek out and see if you're there?"

"They won't."

"I'm not taking that chance."

Violet lifted her chin, the closest she ever came to getting sassy. "I don't know where else to go, Sterling. It's the best place to hide, and you know it."

Beckett was silent during the exchange, watching them from beneath the brim of his cowboy hat. "Actually, the safest place is right here."

"Why?" Sterling was open to any suggestions.

"Since Claude already sent men out here and didn't find the women, why would he look again?"

"True. Unless the ranch hands talk about the women."

Beckett's expression turned hard, and he spat out his piece of hay. "Don't worry about the fellas. I'll keep them in line."

Violet's brow creased with distress. "I couldn't impose on you. I've already done enough."

Sterling glanced at the house. Beckett's idea was actually a good one. Claude's men wouldn't have a reason to return to the Noble Ranch and search again. If they did, Sterling would be here to protect the women. He would have to stick close to the house, but that was better than riding up to the cabin—which was what he would need to do since there was no way he was letting Violet and Hyacinth go up there alone.

Of course, if anyone discovered Violet and Hyacinth were living at his house, he'd still have the pesky gossip and rumors to worry about. But having that was better than leaving the two to fend for themselves.

Sterling hadn't planned on spending more time with Violet, but it looked like he had no other option. He met Beckett's gaze. "It's the most logical plan."

"Yep."

"No." Violet's protest wasn't adamant, and she was easy to sway. He ought to know. He'd influenced her to get engaged and married to him even though she hadn't been ready. But he didn't want to push her into something again. He wanted her to agree to the plan and see the wisdom in it.

Depending on how badly the house had been ransacked, he would need help cleaning it up. He could offer to hire Violet to assist with the task, although she would likely tell him she would do it without pay because it was her fault the men had come there in the first place.

In fact, with Jo-Jo gone and no housekeeper or maid to help with anything, the house had already been in need of a good cleaning. What if he asked her to be the housekeeper until she was safe again and found another living arrangement apart from her father?

"I'll hire you to fill in for Jo-Jo." The words tumbled

out in a rush. "You—and Hyacinth—can cook and clean and do the laundry and all the other things that have been neglected. Hyacinth can do the more active work, and you can stick to the responsibilities that are easier until your ankle heals."

Violet's pretty lips stalled against more protest, and she cocked her head, as though she was giving his suggestion serious consideration.

"I won't pressure you into it. But I will pay you a fair wage, and it would be a great help to me."

"I wouldn't expect a wage."

"I'll pay you what we pay Jo-Jo."

"We'll do it for room and board."

"And a wage."

Hyacinth released a sigh of exasperation. "We'll take the wage along with room and board."

Violet shook her head. "No, Hyacinth. I don't feel right about that."

"It's fair enough. And besides, we need to save for our own place."

Violet fell silent and studied her sister's face. Finally, turned her gaze upon Sterling. "You know you're a stubborn man, don't you?"

He didn't respond, instead waiting for her to make up her mind.

Her eyes softened and filled with gratitude. "I'll accept your offer. Thank you, Sterling."

"Then let's go." A sudden urgency prodded him. "Let's get you both into the house before anyone sees you here."

He'd done the right thing in offering her the job. It would keep her safe for the time being. If only he knew how to keep himself safe. If only he didn't have the niggling feeling that he might all too easily fall for her and get his heart broken again.

A broken heart was the last thing he wanted, because one heartbreak had been enough to last a lifetime.

"You don't need to carry me, Sterling." Violet held up a hand to stop Sterling from scooping her into his arms and carrying her into the house.

She'd gotten back onto the sled and let him pull her to the doorstep. But now that she was on her feet again, she wanted to make her own way.

"You're not walking." Sterling's tone held a familiar note of stubbornness.

Beckett and Hyacinth were watching their interaction. Beckett had already dismounted, and Hyacinth had taken off her skis when they'd reached the end of the field, since the ranch yard was a myriad of mud puddles amidst clumps of dirty snow.

Beckett raised a brow at Sterling as if to question his insistence.

Sterling glared back. "She has to stay off her ankle."

"She has a crutch." Beckett looked pointedly at the simple stick.

"She can use her crutch when I'm not around."

Beckett rolled his eyes.

Sterling gave the ranch foreman an irritated look, then, before Violet could offer any more protest, he lifted her into his arms and started up the slushy path to the back door that led into the kitchen. His breath was warm against her cheek and his arms all too strong.

"I'll be fine, Sterling," she whispered, although weakly. Yes, she wanted to be independent, but she liked being in his arms, liked being pressed against his chest, liked the closeness of his face to hers.

"The more you can stay off your ankle, the quicker it will heal."

Was he saying that because he wanted her to be back on her feet so he could get her out of his life? Or was he truly concerned about her well-being?

She didn't want to ask, wanted instead to cherish each moment of closeness while it lasted. Because all too soon she would be walking again, and he would be busy with his life and no longer interested in hers.

Hyacinth opened the door for them, and as they stepped inside, Sterling stopped abruptly and swept his gaze over the destruction. The chairs had been overturned. The drawers in the hutch were on the floor, their contents spilled. Several crocks had been smashed and the wood bin upended.

A strange sense of despair sifted through Violet. All of this had happened because of her and Hyacinth. If they hadn't sought out Sterling, he wouldn't have to worry about taking care of her and having his home attacked. He could get back to running his ranch and saving his sick cattle.

"I'm so sorry, Sterling." She struggled against him, suddenly needing some distance from him.

He started through the kitchen without releasing her. His expression held wariness, and his eyes were alert, as if preparing for more danger.

"Please, put me down." She couldn't stop the waver in her voice. "I've been nothing but an inconvenience to you since the moment I showed up."

"You're not an inconvenience." His tone was clipped as he moved into the hallway on the other side of the kitchen.

"I've caused you so much trouble."

He halted again and glanced down at her. Although his brow was furrowed, his eyes were a warm brown. "Do you want to know the truth, Violet?"

Even though her stomach quavered at the prospect of what he might say, she nodded. "Yes, please be honest."

"I'm relieved you're here with me."

"You are?"

His eyes held a sincerity she'd always appreciated

about him. "I don't want you anywhere near Claude and his men. If they're capable of doing this to me for sheltering you, then there's no telling what else they could do, especially to you and Hyacinth."

Violet couldn't hold back a shudder. Sterling was right. Claude was more dangerous than she'd realized. What would the saloon owner do if Father wasn't able to pay back his debt some other way?

"I don't understand why Claude is so determined to have the debt repaid. Surely it must be a common occurrence to have men run out of money and be unable to pay what they owe."

Sterling shifted to take in the dining room, which appeared untouched. "I would imagine most men can only afford to gamble a few dollars at a time, not enough to get them into trouble."

"My father was likely gambling with much higher stakes. Maybe that's why he stole from the bank, because he wanted more gambling money."

"My guess is that your father owes too much for Claude to overlook."

"You're probably right."

"If he lets your father get away with not paying, then not only will he lose the money, but he'll lose his reputation and start having more problems with men placing bets they can't afford."

"So he has to send a message to everyone not to mess with him?"

"Exactly." Sterling took several more steps, then paused in front of the parlor.

The intruders had been there, tipping over most of the furniture. But from what she could tell, nothing looked broken. That didn't make up for the mess, but at least it could be picked up.

Hyacinth's footsteps echoed in the hallway behind them, and Beckett's heavier ones followed hers. Beckett seemed to think the living arrangement would work. But what would Mr. and Mrs. Noble think once they heard she was here?

Mr. and Mrs. Noble probably didn't like her anymore. Not after the way she'd hurt Sterling. They were likely relieved she'd left the high country and hoped she would never return. Now Sterling would have to write to them and let them know that not only was she back in his life, but he'd hired her to be their housemaid.

"Your parents will hate me all the more now."

Sterling, who had just started toward the stairs, halted. He narrowed his eyes on Violet. "My parents don't hate you."

She should have kept her comment to herself. But now that it was out, they may as well finish the conversation about the wedding. "Of course they hate me, Sterling. And I don't blame them at all. I embarrassed them, caused a scandal, and ruined all of your mother's wedding plans."

After they'd gotten engaged, Mrs. Noble had offered to have the wedding at the ranch so they could have more space for guests. She'd also planned a wedding dinner to take place after the ceremony. In the couple of weeks leading up to the wedding, the dear woman had spent a great deal of time and money to prepare for the wedding as well as the dinner.

Of course, Violet had helped, and so had Mother and Hyacinth. They'd spent hours at the ranch decorating and preparing and cleaning. But the bulk of the work had fallen upon Mrs. Noble's shoulders.

As sweet as the woman had been, how could Mrs. Noble forgive Violet for ruining so much and embarrassing her in front of all her friends?

Sterling studied Violet's face in the dim lighting of the front hallway. "My parents don't hate you at all, Violet. They weren't even angry. Just sad…for me, for us, for what could have been…"

She studied his face in return, appreciating the sincerity in his eyes. "Your parents are good people, much better than my father."

"Don't give up hope for him. Maybe with all that's happened, he'll finally realize the mess he's made of his life and yours."

Violet could only hope so, but after the years of empty promises he'd made to Mother, how could she ever trust him again?

Sterling started up the stairs. "Since Jo-Jo's room off the kitchen has a single bed, you and Hyacinth can stay in Scarlet's room. The bed there is bigger."

"I don't know if that's right. We're not family."

"It's just a room."

"But we're just maids."

Sterling expelled a long sigh. "No, you're not just maids."

What did he mean by that? The question almost slipped off her tongue, but she swallowed her curiosity because she was too afraid to hear what he might say.

"We'll be fine downstairs, Sterling. Really."

"I insist. Besides, no one else is home now, so it doesn't matter."

He was home, and his room was across the hall. That mattered, didn't it? Not that he would ever do anything to compromise her. Sterling was an honorable man with strong self-control. Maybe she was worrying for nothing. After all, they'd stayed together in the cabin and hadn't had any issues. Why would they now?

He continued up the stairs, holding her as if she weighed nothing, as if he intended to carry her around forever. She knew that wasn't possible, but she couldn't keep from wishing they'd had a little more time last spring to get to know each other—to become more comfortable with each other and to trust one another.

If she'd had that time, would she have married

Sterling in the summer? Or even the autumn? If she'd gone through with the wedding, she wouldn't be in this predicament. Instead, she'd probably be living in the house that Sterling had been planning to build on a plot of land near the main house but far enough away to give them privacy.

The blueprints had been drawn up and the money saved for the building materials, and he'd planned to have a house-raising event when the weather warmed up and the snow thawed. Until then, they'd decided to live with his parents, and she'd assured Sterling she didn't mind, that she was even looking forward to getting to know his mom and Scarlet better.

If she'd had a home with Sterling, Mother and Hyacinth could have stayed with her when the trouble with Father had worsened. Maybe Mother wouldn't have gotten sick. Maybe she would even still be alive.

As Sterling started down the hallway and they passed by the bedrooms, it was clear the men had vandalized upstairs too, dumping drawers and upending more furniture.

"I'm sorry, Sterling," she whispered again, the despair settling over her at not only the destruction now, but at how she'd destroyed the life she could have had with Sterling.

"We'll figure it out," he whispered in return.

She just hoped he was right but had the feeling that some things in life—like her relationship with Sterling— were too broken to be repaired.

14

"We probably shouldn't be rearranging the room, Violet." Hyacinth stood back from the settee she'd moved to the opposite side of the fireplace.

"It's part of the job." At least, that's what Violet had been telling herself.

Sterling and Beckett had done the heavy lifting of righting the furniture before they'd left. Then she and Hyacinth had spent most of the afternoon sweeping and picking up belongings, primarily in the kitchen and pantry and in the bedrooms.

Now that the house was in order, Hyacinth had suggested they work in the parlor first. But Hyacinth's idea of *work* and Violet's were different.

Hyacinth fisted a hand on her hip. "Sterling hired us to clean the house, not to rearrange and redecorate."

"I'm sure he won't mind." Sterling had always seemed to appreciate her decorating abilities, like at the cabin when he'd humored her by finding all the supplies she'd requested.

Violet rested on the piano bench as she surveyed the newest position of the settee and the two wingback chairs. This placement was better than the previous one, which had been too contained and not open enough.

The trouble was that now they needed an end table to go between the two wingback chairs to balance out the settee. Preferably a round pedestal table. And a lamp, one with a light-blue shade that matched the damask upholstery.

Of course, Mrs. Noble didn't have that kind of lantern. But in one of the bedrooms there was a lamp with a pretty, glass shade containing silver threads. Surely Mrs. Noble wouldn't care if they moved it to the parlor. If she didn't like the changes when she returned in the spring, Violet would help to move things back to their original places.

Unless she was gone by then…

She pinched her arm.

"What are you doing?" Hyacinth asked with a pointed glance at Violet's arm.

"Making sure I'm not dreaming."

Hyacinth turned her head away, but not before Violet caught sight of her smile.

"What's so funny?"

Hyacinth faced Violet, this time letting her smile free.

"I told you that you're still in love with him."

Violet didn't have to ask who Hyacinth was referring to. "No, I just can't believe Sterling agreed to let us stay here. That's all."

"I think he's starting to let himself love you again too."

Violet's pulse leaped at her sister's declaration. Was Hyacinth right? Did Sterling still have feelings for her?

There had been a few times since the candy-eating incident that she'd felt him looking at her with interest— or at least, it hadn't been irritation. They'd come a long way from his ordering her off the front porch earlier in the week and telling her he never wanted to see her again to now hiring her to be a maid.

Violet pushed herself up from the bench. "I don't want to let myself think about what he's feeling." Because what if she were wrong? What if he was still just being nice like he would to anyone in need?

"I scolded him for being a coward." Hyacinth's smile faded, and her brow furrowed. "Do I need to scold you now too?"

"That isn't why Sterling hired us, so that he and I could fall in love with each other."

"Sure it is."

Violet opened her mouth to contradict Hyacinth but couldn't formulate a response.

"He wants you. All he needs is a little encouragement,

a nudge in the right direction." Hyacinth paused, tapped her chin, then nodded. "A kiss. That will do it."

"Hy-a-cinth!" Violet couldn't hold back the surprise at her sister's boldness. Even if Violet had thought about the kisses she'd once shared with Sterling, that didn't mean she wanted to kiss him again, did it? No, of course not. "I will not kiss Sterling."

Hyacinth shrugged. "It was obvious the last day in the cabin that the attraction between you two is alive and well."

"No." Embarrassment rushed through Violet. "That's not true."

"He fed you candy."

Violet buried her face in her hands. It had been a charged incident, and she should have known Hyacinth would bring it up.

"And he can't keep his hands off you."

"What?" Violet's head shot up.

Hyacinth was needlessly adjusting one of the pieces of furniture as though she hadn't just spoken crass words.

"Don't say such things, Hyacinth."

"It's true. He carried you far more often than he needed to."

Had he?

Violet glanced at the door to make sure Sterling wasn't standing out in the hallway and listening to their conversation, which was going from bad to worse very quickly.

"He knows I'll kill him if he hurts you again." Hyacinth spoke the words casually as she brushed the armrest of the settee.

Violet gasped. "Kill him? Hyacinth, you're too much."

Hyacinth paused and rolled her eyes. "I'm jesting. Well, not really. I will make him pay if he hurts you. But I don't think he will this time."

A tremor wavered through Violet's stomach. Was it hope? Did she dare believe Hyacinth? "I don't know. Maybe you're making too much of everything."

Hyacinth shrugged and then plopped down onto the settee. "After watching him the past three days…"

Violet held her breath and waited for Hyacinth to say more.

"Like I said, it's obvious he still wants you."

The hope inside Violet made another wave, this one bigger. "What if you're wrong?"

"Kiss him and find out."

And here they were. Back at the kiss again. Even though she could feel the heat creeping up into her cheeks, she ignored it. Hyacinth's request was absurd. Wasn't it?

"It won't hurt anything," Hyacinth offered.

Did she dare? Violet's muscles tensed at such a bold move. She couldn't. "It wouldn't be right to stir things up."

"They're already stirred."

"Not a lot."

"Enough."

Violet blew out a breath. "No, Hyacinth. I will not kiss Sterling."

"Too bad." She hopped back up. "It might make him realize how strong his feelings for you still are."

Violet paused her rambling thoughts. Would a kiss really awaken him to his feelings? And would he be willing to give her a second chance?

"At the very least, it would make it clear to him that you're still interested in him too."

Was she interested?

Emotions swirled up like a rising flood—emotions she didn't want to think about.

Using her crutch, she started toward the settee. "Can we just put aside all this talk about Sterling and focus instead on our work?"

"You know I won't let it go."

"At least for now?"

"As long as you promise you'll give him a fair chance this time."

"You heard what he said about having a different future wife."

"He wanted you to be his wife once. He'll realize you're the one he wants again."

"You can't say that. Now, let's focus. We need a

pedestal table. Could you please search the house and find one?"

As Hyacinth headed out of the room, she grumbled under her breath about the cleaning versus decorating again. But Violet refused to let her sister's more practical nature interfere with the opportunity to transform the room into something truly special.

Violet shifted several decorations and then stood back again. The settee was slightly off-center. She laid her crutch on it and then began to nudge it.

"What are you doing?" Sterling's voice came from the doorway, irritated and accusatory.

She startled, then stumbled. To keep from falling, she grabbed the edge of the settee.

His footsteps thudded rapidly across the room, and before she could sit down, he was lifting her up into his arms.

She would absolutely die of mortification if he'd heard any part of her conversation with Hyacinth from a few minutes ago.

"Did you just come into the house?" She tried to keep her voice nonchalant.

"Yes, and it's a good thing I did, so that I could put an end to whatever you were doing."

Relief made her weak, and she sagged against him.

He situated her against his chest and glared down at her. "You shouldn't be lifting heavy furniture. Not with your injury."

"I was just pushing it a tiny bit." She tried to speak sternly, but her voice came out breathy.

"If I remember right, the settee was on the opposite side of the room." He cocked his head toward where it used to be located. "And now it's here."

She couldn't hold back a laugh.

His brow furrowed even more. "That's no laughing matter. You need to stay off your injured foot."

"Hyacinth moved it, not me." She swallowed the rest of her humor and couldn't stop herself from lifting a hand to his forehead, where she gently fingered the lines, trying to smooth out his worry. Apparently her conversation with her sister was making her bolder and giving her permission to touch Sterling more freely.

The lines didn't go away. But the fierceness of his glare began to dissipate. "You're doing too much."

"I'm being careful."

"Not enough."

This time she lifted her hands to the brim of his cowboy hat and tilted it up just slightly so that she could see his eyes more clearly.

The brown was filled with a concern that went straight to her heart and seemed to ease some of the tightness there. Had her father ever looked at her with such concern? Had he ever taken such tender care of her?

If she'd once been afraid of Sterling being like her father, maybe it was time to see all the ways he was different instead of finding all the ways he was similar.

"Thank you for caring about my injury, Sterling." She loved the feeling of his strong arms holding her up and his broad chest sheltering her.

Hyacinth's words echoed in the back of her mind. *All he needs is a little encouragement, a nudge in the right direction. A kiss.*

She'd told Hyacinth that she wouldn't. But was Hyacinth right? Should she find out if he wanted more?

She'd never initiated a kiss with him in the past, had always waited for him to ask.

She moved her hand from his hat to his jaw and let her fingers graze along the hard line leading away from his chin. This exploration of his face was new territory, and she liked the solidness and the scruff and the nearness.

He grew immobile, hardly breathing.

What was he thinking? That she was being too forward?

She didn't want to meet his gaze and see any sign of rejection there. Instead, she closed her eyes, slid a hand to the back of his neck, then tugged him down at the same time that she leaned forward and touched her lips to his.

He sucked in a sharp breath. Was it one of surprise or distaste?

She was half tempted to pull back in mortification and to apologize and make an excuse. But was Hyacinth right, that she was being a coward in holding back from

Sterling? The truth was, she loved so many things about him and always had. She loved that he was strong-willed and a natural leader while also being gentle and concerned about those weaker than him. She loved his faithfulness, kindness, and sweetness in so many things.

Yes, she may as well finally admit the truth. She loved Sterling Noble. Though she may have run away from him and tried not to love him, here she was again. She loved him too much to give him up.

She needed to win him back. That was ultimately why she was here. And if a kiss would help show him what she felt, then so be it.

Without loosening her hold behind his neck, she angled into the kiss more fully, meshing her mouth to his. At the same time, warmth fanned to life inside her—all the desire for Sterling that had always been there but that she'd tried to forget. It flamed into a fire that she couldn't ignore—one she didn't want to ignore.

His lips were pliable and soft against hers but hesitant.

It didn't matter if he wasn't sure about the kiss or her. She would kiss for both of them.

She dug her fingers into the curling strands at the back of his neck and tried to drag him closer, needing him, needing more.

He shifted and seemed ready to pull away. His lips left hers for an instant, then he groaned, and in the next instant, his mouth collided with hers in an explosion of two worlds that had been torn apart but were now finding their missing places again.

His lips moved in an almost desperate rhythm, as if he was afraid the moment would come to an end too soon and he wouldn't get enough.

His desperation only stoked a frenzy inside her. She matched the give and take of her mouth to his, just as eager to get as much as she could.

The kiss was unlike any they'd shared previously. It held a passion and urgency that had never been there in their few simple, chaste kisses, which had mostly taken place at the front door when she'd been saying goodnight to Sterling.

This intensity was new, and the fire was hot. Though she had the feeling it would be very easy to get burned, she didn't want to think about that. Instead, she wanted Sterling to know how much she cared, how much she desired him, how much she wanted something between them.

As if she'd spoken her thoughts aloud, Sterling abruptly broke their kiss and pulled back. Even before she could open her eyes, he was lowering her to the settee. His movements were hasty and jerky, and as soon as she was out of his arms, he pivoted and stalked to the door.

He was moving so quickly that she expected him to leave the room without a word and without looking back. But as he reached the door, he halted. He blew out a taut breath then shot her a dark look, one she couldn't read. "We can't...I can't..."

She couldn't move, couldn't think about anything but his mouth against hers.

He glanced away, exhaled another breath. "We can't do that again." Then without another word, he exited the room, his footsteps heavy and determined.

Was he determined never to love her again?

Her heart tumbled, and the passion and thrill from the kiss fell away.

She stared at the open doorway, at the emptiness of the front hallway. A moment later, the back door of the house slammed closed.

As silence settled over the parlor, all that remained was an empty ache inside her chest. She'd tried to give him her love, tried to show him she cared, and he'd rejected what she was offering.

He didn't want her. He was finished with her. Even though he'd forgiven her, he was making it clear he had no desire to renew a relationship and intended to move on.

The pain inside her heart reared up into her throat, and tears stung the backs of her eyes.

Was this how he'd felt when she'd walked away from him?

More likely his pain had been a hundred times worse—even a thousand times worse—at what she'd done. The two couldn't even begin to compare because he'd only walked away from a kiss and an invitation to have a relationship again, but she'd walked away from their wedding and a life together.

No wonder he'd been angry when she'd unexpectedly shown up in his life again. It had been callous of her to think she could do so. He would have been better off if she'd stayed away and not reminded him of all that had happened.

She lowered her head and finally let the tears come. She'd hurt him so deeply. How could she ever make up for that?

Maybe she never would, but one thing was certain— she wanted to try. She would do her best to care about him and love him without expecting anything in return. That was all she could do. Then, when her time at the Noble Ranch was over, she would go on her way, give him the freedom he wanted, and never seek him out again.

15

He'd kissed Violet with a kiss that surpassed all other kisses.

Sterling leaned his head against the stall rail and tried to drag in a breath, but he couldn't get air into his lungs. He hadn't been able to draw in a full breath since walking out of the house an hour ago.

Thatcher stood in the haymow with pestle and mortar, the rest of his vaccination supplies spread out on a makeshift table. The process of administering the vaccine was laborious since he had to crush each vaccine individually, mix it with water, then pour it into a glass funnel with a linen filter. From there it was placed into a syringe and injected into the steer's shoulder.

Sterling had been trying to pay attention to the veterinarian's explanation about the steers and the vaccines and what he'd accomplished over the past few days. But the only thing going through Sterling's head was a replay of the kiss and every single second with Violet from the moment she'd gently caressed the furrow in his brow, run her finger along his jaw, then tangled her fingers into his hair.

Each touch had been like striking flint, sending sparks flying in the air. Then she'd arched up, and before he'd realized what she was doing, her lips had met his warmly, firmly, and then begun moving passionately.

He'd tried to hold himself back. But the sparks had set him aflame in an instant, and he'd burned with the need to kiss her back, almost as if he'd had no choice. As if she had power over him and he was helpless to do anything but be swept away with her.

He pressed his thumbs into his eyes to block out the image of her beautiful flushed face and her green eyes peering up at him with desire. But the image wouldn't go away. It was seared into his mind.

Why had she kissed him?

He thought he'd made it clear that he didn't want to consider a future with her again. He'd kept a respectable distance, hadn't flirted, and hadn't encouraged her in any way. Did she think his inviting her to live on the ranch and be the maid meant he was interested in more?

Of course, he would always think she was stunning and desirable and incredible. But he'd already tried a relationship with her once, had even tried to marry her. And it hadn't worked.

They'd both made mistakes. He realized that now. And he'd apologized for his role in all that had gone wrong in their relationship. But he didn't want to pursue her again. How many times did he need to tell himself that?

"Are you listening, boss?" Beckett's voice cut through Sterling's internal battle.

Sterling lifted his head from the stall rail and glanced first at the steer that had been brought inside to be vaccinated, then to Beckett and Thatcher.

Thatcher was a fair-haired man with the stocky build of a Midwestern farmer who was used to working the land. Growing up on a farm had given him firsthand knowledge of livestock in addition to his college training in veterinary school. Sterling wasn't sure why the fellow had moved to their remote part of Colorado, but he wasn't complaining. He liked Thatcher's compassion and helpfulness and determination.

Even if the vaccine didn't end up stopping the blackleg and only slowed its spread, at least Thatcher had done everything humanly possible to help.

"You're mighty distracted." Beckett was leaning against the opposite stall, one boot hooked on a rung, waiting to lead the newly vaccinated steer to a holding area with other beeves that were being monitored for reactions to the vaccine.

"Sorry." Sterling scrubbed a hand down his jaw and

chin, the thick layer of stubble in need of a shave. But the movement only reminded him of Violet's touch on his jaw and the heat she'd left in her wake.

Beckett's eyes narrowed upon Sterling. "You kissed her, didn't you?"

Sterling avoided his foreman's gaze, not sure how to answer the question. Should he admit the truth and risk Beckett scolding him? Or should he lie and deny it with the hope of avoiding a confrontation?

"Dad-blame-it." Beckett's voice dripped with censure. "You did."

Looked like Beckett had answered the question for him. The man was too insightful and could usually read Sterling well.

"What did you go and do a stupid thing like that for?" Beckett pushed away from the stall and tipped up the brim of his hat.

It had been *really* stupid.

Thatcher, in the middle of grinding the vaccine with the mortar, paused and raised his brow.

Sterling ignored the veterinarian and fixed a glare on Beckett. "Thought we were keeping things private."

"Reckon we're private here, right, Thatcher?" Beckett's voice, though casual, also held a veiled threat.

"Very private." Thatcher began the tedious process of crushing a new batch of the vaccine. "Although, you should know that when I was in town last night at the livery, stitching up a horse, I got a question or two about how Sterling had skied out to a cabin he owns to help out the Berkley women."

Sterling's backbone stiffened. His helping the women was supposed to remain a secret.

Beckett spat the hay out of his mouth and took a menacing step toward Thatcher, as if the veterinarian were to blame for spreading the word.

Thatcher stopped grinding and held up both hands, one grasping the pestle. "Don't look at me. I didn't say anything. I pretended I didn't know what the folks at the livery were talking about."

Sterling's pulse began to tap harder. How had people learned he'd gone out to the cabin to help Violet and Hyacinth? When they realized he was back, would they also suspect that he'd brought the women home with him?

"I didn't have to pretend too hard, though." Thatcher paused again in his grinding. "I really don't know much about the two women except that Claude St. Germaine claims they're his dancehall girls."

"They're not his dancehall girls." Sterling practically spat the words, disgusted by the mere thought, let alone the actual reality.

"Just telling you what's being spread around town."

Inwardly, Sterling cursed at whoever had started the rumors.

Beckett stood rigidly now, his hand on his revolver. "What do you want me to do, boss? Want me to take a couple of the fellows and ride into town and give Claude a lesson that he shouldn't be claiming stuff that doesn't belong to him?"

Sterling didn't know a whole lot about Beckett's past life before he'd come to Colorado. The foreman had been pretty tight-lipped about it, had only shared that he'd worked on a ranch somewhere in the South and had the experience necessary to be a foreman. It was at times like this that Sterling suspected Beckett had a complicated—maybe even a rough—history, one that made him unafraid to go head-to-head with Claude's men, no matter how vicious they might be.

Sterling would like nothing better than to ride with Beckett and confront Claude too. But he didn't want Beckett or any of his other ranch hands to get in trouble. Because such a conflict would cause lots of trouble, and people would end up getting hurt.

Sterling shook his head. "Best to start off on the cautious side and handle this without violence first."

"That's not what Claude did when he messed up your house."

Beckett was right. Claude's men hadn't needed to upend things the way they had in looking for Violet and Hyacinth. Most likely they'd done it to make a point to Sterling that he wasn't safe as long as he was sheltering the women.

Even so, he wasn't ready to get dirty with them. "We're not going to lower ourselves to their standard and break the law."

"I can send them a message without breaking the law."

"I'm sure you can. But let's wait—"

"Wait for Claude to send his men again? And this time get the women?"

"If they come back, we won't hesitate to defend ourselves."

"And chance the women getting hurt?"

Sterling's muscles tightened at the prospect of that happening.

Beckett's expression was stormy, and Sterling had no doubt his own was the same way. The danger to the women was imminent. Did he want to have a battle here on the ranch? Or would it be better to ride into town and let the conflict play out there?

"If I may interject here," Thatcher said as he began to pour water into a glass beaker.

Sterling nodded, not sure what the veterinarian could offer in terms of viable advice in this volatile situation. But Sterling was open to any ideas that could keep the women safe.

Thatcher finished with the water, then lifted the beaker and poured it into the crushed vaccine. "Sounds like you still love her."

"No." Sterling growled the word. "Not anymore—"

"But you just kissed her?" Thatcher paused his work and cast a raised brow at Sterling.

Shoot. He didn't want to admit she'd been the one to kiss him first. If that word got out, her reputation might become tarnished. He didn't want men thinking she was easy or that he was taking advantage of her.

Thatcher picked up a stirring stick and began mixing the solution. "Why would you kiss her unless you still have feelings for her?"

Obviously Thatcher, though he was fairly new to Summit County, had heard about his failed wedding to Violet. What was the point in denying he had some feelings for Violet? He would only be lying to them and himself. "Fine. I do care about her—"

"Oh, really." Beckett's comment was laced with sarcasm.

"But I don't love her."

Thatcher poured his mixture into the filter and the funnel above the syringe. "Plenty of marriages have started on a lot less than you have with her."

He was likely referring to the mail-order brides that were on their way for both him and Beckett. Except for a few letters exchanged, the two men would hardly know their brides when they got married.

"What's your point?" Beckett crossed his thick arms as if daring Thatcher to say anything more about marriage.

Thatcher wasn't looking at Beckett, was instead focused on getting every drop of the vaccine into the syringe. "My point is that the best way to keep Violet safe is for Sterling to marry her."

Beckett's gaze turned stormier—if that were possible. And Sterling couldn't speak past the surprise lodged in his throat.

Thatcher was too busy to look Sterling's way as he shook the funnel, tapped the tube, and patted the filter.

Marry Violet? No, Sterling absolutely wouldn't consider that again. Ever.

He couldn't. Could he?

Beckett shook his head as if sensing the question.

No, it was impossible. He'd already tried marrying her once, and it hadn't worked out. He wasn't willing to take that risk again. Some other man would have to marry her. But who? Who could he suggest for her?

His mind raced with the options. Was there anyone in Breckenridge or Summit County he would be willing to entrust her to?

He pushed aside one name and face after another of the men he knew. On such short notice, he couldn't think of a single man. Besides, even if he could narrow it down to a decent fellow, what would happen to Hyacinth? She would still be in danger.

Thatcher paused, the syringe upright and ready for the steer. He lifted a brow at Sterling. "Well?"

"It wouldn't work."

"With your reaction to that kiss, I have the feeling it'd work out just fine." Thatcher flashed him a grin before stepping up to the steer, looping an arm around its neck, and then jabbing the needle into the creature's shoulder.

The steer snorted and tried to step backward, but Thatcher had a tight hold. "It's all right, fellow," he said softly.

Although Sterling wanted to be irritated with the veterinarian for his assumptions and for poking his nose into business that wasn't his, he clamped his mouth closed. He owed Thatcher too much gratitude for his tireless help with the herd. And the truth was, Thatcher had offered a logical plan for keeping Violet safe.

It just wasn't one Sterling wanted to use.

"Anyway," Thatcher said as he finished injecting the shot. "Just something to think about."

Before Sterling could say anything else, Beckett cocked his head to the door.

It was the sign Beckett wanted a private conversation. And of course Sterling knew what his foreman was going to tell him.

As they stepped out into the fading afternoon, Sterling once again scanned the ranch yard and the lane leading toward the main road. They'd stationed a ranch hand near the gate to keep watch for anyone who might be coming from town to pay them a visit.

But would Claude's men come openly, or would they try to sneak in from the back route along the Blue River? Sterling hadn't wanted to take away another ranch hand to post a man there. But now that Claude knew they were sheltering the women, Sterling might not have a choice.

Beckett was surveying the land too, obviously realizing Claude's men would be back. When they returned, they would probably be prepared for a fight.

"You can't marry her." Beckett's statement was matter-of-fact.

"I knew you'd say that."

"That's because I saw how she destroyed you."

"I'm still alive and breathing."

"You were like a dead man walking for weeks after she left you."

"I'm fine now." What was he doing arguing about the matter? He wasn't planning to marry Violet, and he needed to let his friend know that.

"That woman is too fickle." Beckett stared at the house with a scowl. "She'll just hurt you again, and you know it."

That's what Sterling feared. As much as the sparks had ignited desire with Violet again, hotter than when they'd been courting, she was fighting fears that were still very real and alive. He understood that now in a way he hadn't before, which was all the more reason not to consider marriage to her again. She would be scared and would have doubts and would be all too ready to run away again at the slightest spook.

He couldn't risk that.

He expelled a breath. "I won't do it."

Beckett blew out a breath too. "Dad-blame-it, Sterling. I know you're gonna do it."

"I said I won't."

"I saw the way you were looking at her when you got home today."

He'd been trying hard to keep from staring at her, but maybe he'd done more looking than he should have. She was just so pretty and so hard to resist.

"It doesn't matter," he offered. "Even if I tell her we ought to get married for her safety, she won't do it."

"I saw the way she was looking at you too."

Sterling's pulse hopped. "How?"

Beckett muttered under his breath and began to walk off.

Sterling didn't blame his friend for his frustration. He would probably be frustrated if the roles were reversed and he could see Beckett heading down the same destructive path as before.

But did it have to be destructive again? Could Sterling love Violet differently this time? He'd already realized he'd been selfish in his desires for her before. What if he could try again and do better?

His heartbeat galloped forward with a strange

anticipation. But just as quickly, he tried to rein it in. He was crazy to give Thatcher's suggestion to marry Violet even a second of consideration, wasn't he?

Yes, he was completely crazy.

He twisted his head first one way and then the other, cracking his bones and trying to loosen the tension in his shoulders.

Even if the idea was far-fetched, it *would* solve the problem of Claude claiming her. In fact, it was an easy solution that would prevent a fight and possible bloodshed. Maybe they could find a husband for Hyacinth too. She was nineteen and old enough to be married.

Stuffing his hands into his pockets, he let his gaze settle back on the house. Time was of the essence. If he was going to implement a marriage plan to thwart Claude, he would have to do it soon, maybe even tonight.

Marry Violet tonight? Or most likely tomorrow morning?

He paced toward the corral then back.

What was wrong with him? He couldn't consider it, mainly because he knew Violet would never follow through with it. Even if she agreed and realized it would keep her safe, when the moment came to say her vows, she would get scared and back out.

Unless…

His pacing came to a halt.

What if he assured her the marriage would be in name only and that she could leave at any time?

He hated both ideas. He didn't want a marriage in name only, and he wouldn't want her to leave him at any time. But would she agree to the plan more readily if she knew she had a way out? Did he want her to agree to the plan?

He closed his eyes and attempted to ward off the truth. But what was the point of denying what was so obvious to everyone, including himself? The truth was he loved Violet. Maybe he'd never stopped loving her. Maybe he'd wanted her all along and would never be satisfied with anyone else. And maybe he was looking for an excuse to have her back in his life.

This marriage of convenience plan would give him that excuse. It would also give him the opportunity to show her he was different now, that he could love her unselfishly without asking for anything in return.

The ache in Sterling's heart pulsed as if to remind him of all the pain he'd already experienced with Violet. Could he pursue a relationship with her, knowing full well she might leave him once more? On the other hand, could he really live the rest of his life knowing he'd had another chance to be with her but had thrown it away?

No matter what choice he made, he was bound to face pain. The real question was whether he could finally make the choice to love her anyway, no matter what happened and no matter how much pain it cost him. Because that was unconditional love—loving when it wasn't easy, even when it was the hardest thing in the world.

He hadn't understood that earlier in the year. Now that he was learning what true sacrificial love meant, could he gather the courage to do what he'd failed at last time?

He wasn't sure. But was it time to try?

16

Violet couldn't sleep.

She stirred the saucepan of warm milk on the stovetop, wishing she could find a way to stop the whirlwind twisting and turning through her mind—the whirlwind that had been there since she'd kissed Sterling earlier.

Oh, the kiss.

She released a blissful sigh, then touched her fingertips to her lips as if in doing so she could feel his kiss again. She closed her eyes and imagined the pressure and passion. Even though he'd run from her afterward, he'd kissed her back with a fervor that had wreaked havoc with her body.

He'd liked it. Maybe not as much as she had. But still, he couldn't have pretended everything—the emotion, the tenderness, the desire.

She'd certainly felt it all. More so than ever before.

Was that because this time she knew she loved him? Had it taken the time away from him, the distance and soul-searching, to realize she would never find another man like him?

She actually wasn't sure if she would ever be the same again after that kiss. So maybe it was a good thing he'd said he wouldn't kiss her again.

Opening her eyes, she stifled a disappointed sigh and stirred the milk again.

She hadn't mentioned the kiss to her sister, but Hyacinth had taken one look at Violet's face when she'd returned to the parlor with the pedestal table, and she'd known. She'd just smiled smugly with an I-told-you-so glint in her eyes.

At the soft tap against the back door, Violet startled. She pivoted to find Sterling entering. The low light from the lantern she'd set on the table didn't quite reach to illuminate his face, but from the stiffness of his shoulders, she knew something was wrong.

She drew her coat closed over her long nightgown. Since she didn't have a robe, she'd donned her coat before leaving the bedroom. Even so, she felt strangely bare, especially with her hair hanging free of the usual constraints.

"I was hoping to see you," he whispered, removing his hat and setting it on the table.

"I couldn't sleep..." She ducked her head, hoping he

wouldn't be able to read her thoughts and realize the reason for her sleeplessness—that she'd been thinking about him and their kiss nonstop.

In fact, her flighty thoughts had gone from replaying their kiss to imagining him in bed. She'd never thought about him in bed before. Maybe she'd had a few moments before her wedding day back in April when she'd felt a little nervous about her wedding night and the mysteries she would discover. But something in the kiss earlier had awoken a need inside her. Now she was embarrassingly curious about what it might be like to lie beside him and kiss him as much as she wanted all night long.

Hopefully the kitchen was shadowed enough that he wouldn't be able to see the mortification rushing into her cheeks.

He twisted the brim of his cowboy hat in his large hands. Was he nervous about something?

What if he'd already changed his mind about having her and Hyacinth working in the house as maids? Maybe he hadn't liked how much she'd started rearranging and changing the decorations.

He hadn't said anything about the furniture except that he hadn't wanted her to exert herself in moving it. Besides, he'd always appreciated her decorating efforts in the past, had always complimented her.

So why was he here? Had he finally come in for the night?

"Would you like some warm milk? It might help you sleep better. Not that you need help sleeping. I'm sure you sleep just fine in your bed." She was rambling and starting to picture him in bed again.

She spun back to the stove, could feel the steam rising from the pan, adding to the warmth in her face. She reached for the ladle and began to scoop milk into the mug she'd readied.

"Sure, I'll take a cup," he offered quietly. "If you have enough."

She would gladly give it all up for him if he needed it. But she couldn't say that. "Of course. You can even take it with you up to your room." She turned and held the mug out to him where he stood, only a couple of feet away.

"Thank you." He'd shed his gloves and now took another step closer and wrapped both hands around the mug. "I'm not going to bed. I'm taking the next shift of guard duty."

"Guard duty?" In the process of reaching for another mug from the open shelf next to the stove, she halted.

"That's what I want to talk to you about."

Her muscles tensed. "Are we in danger again?"

He released a tense breath. "Seems word spread that I was hiding you and Hyacinth at the miner's cabin."

"Oh." Had someone seen her and Hyacinth leaving on the skis that day and guessed where they were going?

Or had someone heard that Sterling had gone out there to help them?

"That means Claude knows I'm helping you and Hyacinth."

At the news, her shoulders sank. "So it's only a matter of time now before he comes back?"

Sterling hesitated. "Once he learns I'm home, yes, I'm guessing he'll send his men back here and try to collect you and Hyacinth."

Violet pressed a hand to her forehead. With her crutch under one arm, her coat fell open, and cold air slipped around her.

Sterling's gaze dropped to her now-visible nightgown, and his Adam's apple fell in a hard swallow.

She glanced down at herself to see that the neckline was low, almost indecently so, especially for a nighttime encounter with Sterling. She rapidly clutched her coat together, then hugged her arms over her chest.

His gaze shifted to her hair, the long strands damp after the bath she and Hyacinth had indulged in before going to bed. His gaze lingered over the dark waves that hung over her shoulder and down her arm.

What was he thinking?

She wasn't sure if he'd ever seen her hair down before. She'd been careful to keep it plaited while he'd been at the cabin. Of course, she hadn't expected a late-night encounter with him in the kitchen. But she supposed anything was possible now that they were living under the same roof. She would have to be more careful in the future.

"You look beautiful," he whispered, still staring at her hair.

A flush splashed through her body, warming her skin and seeping all the way to a place deep inside. "I didn't expect to see anyone…"

"I'm sorry for surprising you." His eyes had darkened. "I saw the light and figured you were awake."

"It's all right."

He hesitated, then he lifted a hand to her hair and touched one of the damp strands.

Her breath hitched.

He caressed the piece of hair tenderly, trailing his fingers down until he reached her wrist. Then he fingered the edge of her sleeve.

She still couldn't breathe.

"Violet," he started quietly.

"Yes?" Was her voice too eager? She had to be careful. She'd almost ruined things with her kiss earlier, and she couldn't risk pushing him away again or upsetting the newfound peace that was developing between them.

As if recognizing the same, he retracted his hand and stuffed it into his trouser pocket. "I've been thinking about how to keep you safe from Claude and your father."

She honestly hadn't thought much about her father since running away earlier in the week. It had been the same way when she'd left Colorado with Mother in the spring. She hadn't missed him then either. He'd never been an integral part of her life. Not the way Mother had been.

Why, then, was she letting his mistakes take up so much room in her ability to love a man? He didn't deserve that space. She needed a way to clean out the clutter so she was free to love another man more completely and wholly, preferably Sterling.

He was still holding the warm milk with one hand. He swished the liquid around, then lifted the mug and took a drink. "As I said, Claude's men will be back."

"I'm sorry, Sterling. This is our fault—"

"No." He spoke the word sharply, then lowered his voice. "No, Violet. Don't say that."

"I don't want to bring more trouble and damage to the ranch. So Hyacinth and I will move out tomorrow."

"That's not why I'm telling you about the danger." He twisted the mug in his hands almost nervously.

Was he nervous about having to ask her to leave? "We'll go in the morning."

"You don't have to leave."

"Yes, we'll find some other place to hide. I'll think about it tonight."

He released a soft growl. Then he set his mug down

on the table before reaching for both of her hands.

As his warm fingers circled hers, she tried not to think about the strength in his touch as well as the gentleness. He was such a mixture of both qualities, and she loved that about him.

"Hear me out." He studied her hands and avoided her gaze.

"Okay."

"I know you won't like the idea. But it's the best one."

She wouldn't like it? She wanted to protest right away, but she had told him she would listen to his plan.

"I think the best thing to do," he started, then stopped and cleared his throat.

He was nervous. That could only mean the plan really was one she wouldn't like. She grew motionless, her heart filling with a whisper of dread.

"It doesn't have to be permanent, and it doesn't have to be real," he rushed to say. "It can be temporary and in name only. And you can leave whenever you want. I won't hold you back. And I promise I won't be upset at you."

What was he talking about?

He chanced a glance up. "What do you think?"

"About what?"

"I'm saying…" He dropped his attention to the floor, his expression etched with embarrassment. "All I'm saying is that if you agree to it, Claude won't come after you."

"Agree to what?" As soon as the words left her mouth she knew.

He was proposing marriage again.

She jerked her hands free from his and took a step back.

"Don't say no right away, Violet." He let his hands fall to his sides.

Her heart started pounding with the speed of a runaway carriage, the same way it had the first time he'd proposed to her.

Sterling's forehead furrowed, as though he could sense her mounting panic.

But why was she panicking? She didn't want fear to be her first reaction to marrying him.

"We'll get married on paper." He spoke calmly and quietly. "But nothing will change between us. We'll pretend for the community and everyone to keep Claude away. Once this is all over, you're free to go. I won't hold you here."

Her runaway pulse began to slow to a normal pace, and she inhaled a full breath. She could handle this situation differently than she had before. Because this time was different. He wasn't asking her to marry him out of love. He was doing it because he was a kind man and wanted to help her out of a dangerous situation.

She breathed out again and let the tension ease from

her shoulders. As she did so, she felt a small stab of disappointment. At herself for her reaction. She obviously still had work to do in overcoming her fears. However, in this moment, she couldn't let those fears stop her from considering Sterling's idea.

He was watching her, his eyes filled with uncertainty. Did he think she was rejecting him again? She had to reassure him that she cared about him, that her hesitancy had more to do with *her* than *him*. Should she just admit she loved him? Would that help? Or would it only make things worse?

Hadn't he indicated that he didn't want to stay married to her, that the arrangement would only be temporary? She hadn't misunderstood him, had she?

"How long would we stay together?" The question wasn't exactly what she wanted to ask, but she wasn't sure how to push deeper and find out how he really felt about it.

He hesitated. "Only as long as necessary to make sure you're safe."

So he really didn't want anything permanent. "So the marriage would be just for show?"

"We would need a ceremony, probably tomorrow morning, to prove that we're married. After that, we won't need to do anything different than what we are now."

Was that what he wanted? To keep her at arm's length?

She tried to study his face in the dim lighting. His eyes were half-lidded and guarded, as though he didn't want her to see into his heart. Why? Because she would see his doubts?

Maybe she just needed to accept that he would never want to be with her again. He'd made that clear enough over the past few days, and especially this afternoon, when he'd told her he didn't want to kiss her again.

All he was doing was helping her, not only with the offer of the maid job but now with the plan to marry her. She had to stop reading more into what he was doing.

Did she want it all to mean more to him? Did she want him to want her?

She shook her head. That wasn't fair to him.

"Don't say no tonight." He held out a hand as if to stop her protest, then took a step toward the back door. "Think about it, and we can talk again in the morning."

He'd mistaken her shaking her head as her opposition to his second proposal? Not that it had been anything like his first proposal. Maybe it couldn't even be considered a proposal. Whatever the case, she couldn't deny his request to at least think about it.

"Okay, I'll think about it."

He released an audible breath.

Was he relieved? Had he hoped she would want to go through with this? What did he have to gain except for a lot of hassle?

He backed up another step. "I'll come for your answer at dawn."

She could only watch as he swiped up his hat, placed it on his head, and then finished crossing to the door. Once the door closed behind him, she grabbed hold of the nearest chair and lowered herself. Her legs and hands were both shaking.

Marry Sterling Noble?

Could she do it this time?

She buried her face in her hands, and the tears came before she could stop them. She wasn't exactly sure why the emotion was so strong or what she was feeling. Maybe surprise. Maybe frustration. Maybe even some fear. All she knew was that her chest was swelling with an overwhelming need to cry.

Gentle hands squeezed her shoulders. Hyacinth's hands.

Had her sister been standing outside the kitchen and listening to the conversation with Sterling? A part of Violet wanted to be upset at Hyacinth's eavesdropping. But another part of her knew she would have had to explain everything to Hyacinth eventually anyway.

Hyacinth gently brushed Violet's loose hair.

Violet blinked back her tears and tried to swallow the swell of emotion. Then she lifted her head and peered up into Hyacinth's green eyes, so much like her own. "What should I do, Hyacinth?"

Hyacinth continued to caress her hair. "You can only do one thing."

"What?"

"You have to marry him."

"Why?" But even as the question slipped out, Violet already knew the answer.

"Because you love him."

Violet nodded. Was it really that simple?

"And because you need to do it to finally overcome your fears."

More tears slid down Violet's cheeks. "But he doesn't want it to be real, and he wants it to only be temporary."

Hyacinth shook her head, her long loose hair swaying. "Maybe he was thinking of the last time and trying not to pressure you into something real and permanent if that's not what you want."

Was that part of it? Violet sniffed back her tears.

"Or maybe he's trying to keep himself from getting hurt again."

"I don't want to hurt him this time."

"Then you'll have to show him that."

"How?" Violet wiped the dampness from her cheeks. "And don't tell me I need to kiss him again."

Hyacinth smirked. "That probably would help. But no, I think the best thing you can do is show him that you've changed, the same way he's trying to show you that he's changed."

"But what can I do to show him?"

"Prove to him that you're done running away from love."

Violet wasn't sure how to do that. But she knew her sister was right. She had to show Sterling she was no longer afraid of love.

But was that true? When the time came tomorrow morning to stand before the reverend and say *I do*, would she be able to do it? Even now, when she knew she loved Sterling?

Sterling approached the house wearily. Now that light was beginning to outline the rocky peaks of the eastern range, it was time to find out Violet's decision about moving forward with a marriage of convenience.

He'd had time to think on the plan throughout the long watches of the night and dark early-morning hours. The truth was, as much as he wanted a real marriage with real love, the only woman he wanted was Violet. She was the only woman he'd ever wanted and always would be. He'd tried to deny that for months, but since the moment she'd walked back into his life, he'd been reminded all over again of how beautiful and kindhearted and creative and sweet she was.

He liked that she cared so much for Hyacinth and was willing to do anything to save her. He liked that Violet was humble and could admit her mistakes and was willing to grow. And he liked that she was easy to talk to and be with and was always adding her flare to everything she touched.

Besides that, she fit so well with him. She wasn't intimidated by his personality and never seemed to cower, even during his most demanding moments. She also had an easygoing way of seeing life that complemented his more driven and compelling outlook. He knew a future with her would never be dull and that she would keep him from getting too stuck in his ways, and he appreciated that about her.

Yes, he loved her. He loved her like he would no other woman. And he was ready and willing to take whatever future she would give him, even if that meant a chaste marriage, even if that meant she never loved him in return, and even if that meant she wasn't interested in a long-term commitment.

Yes, he wanted more. He wanted everything with her. But he would also be happy having her whether he earned her love in return or not.

Oh, he planned to try to win her. He would spend his life trying to win her. But regardless of what happened, he would love her and cherish her as long as she would let him.

A light glimmered in the parlor window.

Was Violet awake at the early-morning hour? Already waiting for him?

He halted.

He'd told her he would come for her answer at dawn. Now that the time was upon them, he wasn't sure he could face her. What if she declined his proposal from last night? Had it even been a proposal? It had been more like a business plan than a heartfelt declaration of love.

Maybe that was okay. Maybe that's what he liked about it—that he could marry her without all the emotion this time and without the fear of her running away. At least, he hoped she wouldn't be afraid, that she would see their arrangement as practical and sensible.

He could marry her first and have the commitment in place, and then he could work on earning her trust. It was a backward way to approach marriage with her, but the frontward way hadn't worked, and this was all he had left.

If he could make himself go inside...

He stared at the softly illuminated front window for a few more seconds before forcing his feet into action, this time heading for the flagstone path that led to the porch. His footsteps seemed to grow heavier, but he made himself go.

He had nothing to lose if she said no. That's what he was telling himself, since she wasn't really his anyway. If she was willing, he would send one of the ranch hands into town to fetch Reverend Livingston. At least at the early-morning hour, the reverend would be home and would hopefully be willing to come out to do the wedding ceremony.

With his pulse tapping a harder rhythm, Sterling bounded up the steps and crossed to the door. As he opened it and stepped inside, his heart pushed up into his throat. He was lying to himself to say that he had nothing to lose. The truth was, he wanted this—her—so badly he could hardly breathe. If she said no now, would he be able to go on?

He closed the front door and leaned against it, his hand still on the door handle. He couldn't bear her rejection again. What was he doing here? He had to leave.

"Sterling?" Her voice came from the parlor. "Is that you?"

He drew in a deep breath. He couldn't leave. He had to persuade her to go through with the marriage to keep her safe from Claude. That was what this was about. It wasn't about him. He couldn't forget it.

He shoved away from the door and forced his feet to cross to the parlor. As he stepped into the doorway, he stopped short.

Violet was standing in the middle of the parlor, attired in a fancy green gown that matched her eyes. The shimmering material hugged her womanly form, showing off every curve of her lovely body. The neckline was daringly low, with velvet lace barely concealing her cleavage. She wore a simple gold necklace with a pearl pendant, which drew attention to the long stretch of her neck and the graceful curve of her chin. Her dark hair was coiled into a fashionable knot with tiny curls cascading around her ears.

His lungs ceased to function, and his mind refused to work. The only thought running through his head was that she was stunning.

As though seeing his scrutiny, she lifted a gloved hand to her necklace. She touched the pearl with trembling fingers before quickly hiding her hand behind her back. "I have an answer for you."

From the corner of his eye, he glimpsed Hyacinth standing at the end of the hallway. She was attired in her best too.

His heart gave an extra beat. Did this all mean what he thought it did?

He allowed himself another step into the room. The golden candles on the mantel had been lit, as had the candelabra on the piano, lending the room a soft, welcoming glow. Had she done this to welcome him?

His heart pattered harder.

With her crutch tucked under one arm, she didn't move from her spot in the center of the room, the light from the candles shining on her and making her hair dark and luxurious. Her chest rose and fell, giving him a tempting glimpse behind the lace to the smooth, generous swell of flesh.

His mouth went dry.

He'd always thought she was more beautiful than any

other woman, but this morning, she was a goddess, and she had the power to command him body, soul, and spirit. He was helpless to do anything but adore her and admire her and long for her.

What would it be like to hold her for as long as he wanted, to kiss every single inch of her skin?

"Would you like to know my decision?" Her voice was soft and shaky.

Was she nervous?

He swallowed the desire that had risen rapidly within him, and he tried to cool his thoughts and corral them from the direction they'd been going, which had been completely selfish and concerned with only his own pleasure instead of how she was feeling and what she needed.

He made himself walk calmly forward across the rug toward her. He would have married her in this room back in April if things had been different between them. Could he keep them going in the right direction now?

Her eyes rounded with each step that he drew nearer. Despite her hurt ankle, she held herself with such poise and beauty that he had a hard time remembering how skittish she was.

Even though he wanted to go to her, wrap her in his arms, and draw her close enough that he could feel the suppleness of her body, he made himself stop an arm's length away.

"Whatever you want to do," he said in a low voice that came out huskier than he'd intended. "I'll respect your decision."

She nodded, visibly swallowed, then lifted her chin. "What I want to do is have a wedding."

He held her gaze for a moment. Was she speaking the truth? Or was she trying to appease him?

"I'm ready, Sterling. I promise." She hobbled closer, lifted a hand as though she wanted to reach for him, but then lowered it and clasped her hands together in front of her.

He closed the distance between them, then tentatively took hold of her hands. "Are you sure?"

"I'm not going to run away this time." Her voice shook.

"But you're thinking about it?"

She hesitated, capturing her bottom lip with her teeth.

He had to glance away, couldn't watch her or he would groan and embarrass himself with his desire for her.

"I admit," she whispered. "I am nervous."

"What would help ease your mind?"

She lifted her face to his, giving him a view of her elegant neck and the exquisite pale skin just waiting to be explored. By him. Only him. He never wanted another man to touch her. He was suddenly insanely jealous at the thought of any man ever touching her. He wouldn't let that happen—not in the dancehall, not anywhere.

She bit her lip again.

Heat spilled through him—a heat that was molten and thick and full of fire.

"Would you kiss me?" she asked softly. "That might help—"

Before she could finish, he bent and touched his lips to hers.

She released a tiny breathy sigh. Of happiness?

Whether happy or not, she'd asked him to kiss her. That had to mean something, didn't it? It had to mean she felt connected to him or at least was still attracted to him.

Her mouth met his hungrily, without any tentativeness, just like the last time they'd kissed.

He couldn't contain his own hunger, which had been building over the hours. He delved in and tasted her, letting himself feast on her lips and giving back to her the feast she was asking for. He loved the give and take of their kiss, loved the forcefulness of her passion, and loved the eagerness with which she savored him in return.

It was almost as if she knew what she wanted and was trying to tell him so. Was it possible she wanted marriage with him, maybe always had, but just wasn't sure how to chase away the demons of her past?

Even as her kiss turned deeper, a warning inside him

told him he had to be patient, had to go slow, and needed to use caution.

A banging at the back of the house startled him, and he broke away from her.

Her hand flittered to her neck then her lips. Her eyes were wide and filled with wonder…and desire.

His heart leaped with hope. He could continue to woo and win her after their wedding, and maybe someday—maybe even soon—she would be ready for more between them than a marriage of convenience.

As it was, he needed to send one of the hired hands after the reverend and get him out to the ranch as soon as possible.

The footsteps in the hallway thudded purposefully and with a slight scuff that told him Beckett had come in, likely to find out the plans for the morning.

Sterling took another step away from Violet, hoping that would prevent his foreman from knowing he'd just kissed Violet again—although Sterling had the feeling it wouldn't work and that Beckett would be able to tell right away.

"Boss?" came Beckett's voice from the doorway behind him. "I'll watch the women while you go get some shut-eye."

Violet was grasping the back of one of the wingback chairs and seemed to be trying to compose herself in front of Beckett.

Sterling met her pretty, wide-eyed gaze. Did she really want to go through with the wedding this morning?

She nodded as though hearing his silent question.

"No sleep for me this morning, Beckett." He held Violet's gaze. "At least, not until after the wedding."

Beckett didn't respond, didn't even move. Regardless, Sterling could feel the foreman's displeasure as if it had walked into the room and taken a seat.

Violet's attention shifted to Beckett, and her brow rose. Hyacinth stood behind the foreman in the hallway, attired in a lovely gown and with her dark hair pulled up stylishly too. Sterling liked that she was so loyal and concerned about Violet, even if she sometimes was overly direct.

Beckett's eyes had narrowed. "So you're going through with marriage even though it's a foolish idea?"

Sterling bristled. "It's the best way forward." He leveled his words and a glare at Beckett.

Beckett glared back. "A wedding only takes care of half the problem. We still have the sister to worry about when Claude sends his men again."

"The *sister* has a name," Hyacinth muttered.

"The *sister*," Beckett said more distinctly, "is probably even more than half the problem."

Hyacinth released a scoffing sound.

Sterling had been thinking about Hyacinth during the long hours of standing watch. And there was only one man he trusted her with. "You're going to marry Hyacinth," he said to Beckett.

The man's dark brows shot up, disappearing under the brim of his cowboy hat. "No how, no way—"

"It'll be temporary."

"I've got a bride lined up."

"She's not coming until the spring."

"It doesn't matter. I'm not gonna risk it."

Sterling had suspected Beckett might say that, because the ranch foreman was a man of honor and wouldn't want to cause problems or disrespect his future bride. "Then you'll get engaged to Hyacinth."

"That's not gonna happen either."

Behind Beckett, Hyacinth was shaking her head. She didn't like the plan any more than he did. But it would help keep her safe, and that was really what mattered most.

"You pretend she's your woman until this blows over."

"And you think an engagement will stop Claude?"

"If he knows she's under your protection, you'll make it clear she's off-limits."

Beckett's mouth stalled around his next response.

"I'm not advocating going over to the Red Cap Saloon and beating up Claude or any of his men." Sterling needed to emphasize again his position on the violence. "But I trust you'll find a lawful way to let them know Hyacinth is your fiancée and that they can't touch her."

This time Beckett didn't protest.

Sterling knew he was dangling the proverbial carrot in front of his foreman—a carrot in the form of intimidating a bully who needed to be put in his place. Beckett wouldn't be able to resist the bait. And how could Sterling oppose Beckett's doing a little intimidating?

"No," came Hyacinth's firm voice from the hallway. "I won't pretend such a thing."

"Please, Hyacinth." Violet crossed to her sister. "It will be better than nothing."

"I'm not lying about being engaged to someone." Hyacinth pressed her lips together in that stubborn way she had.

Beckett stepped back into the hallway and was now facing Hyacinth. He was taking her in slowly, probably deciding if she was worth the hassle. Of course, Hyacinth didn't have Violet's delicate beauty, but she was definitely a fine-looking woman.

With her more serious outlook on life, Hyacinth was jaded and sarcastic and too much like Beckett. The two would never make a good match in real life. But for a couple of months, until after the new year, they could pretend to have a relationship. What harm could come of that?

"Beckett's a nice man," Violet said.

"No, he's not." Hyacinth raised her freckled nose at Beckett, her green eyes flashing with disdain.

"Now, hold on." Sterling needed to steer the conversation in a different direction before Beckett took offense and stalked off without agreeing to the plan.

Before Sterling could formulate something positive to say, Beckett, who was still staring at Hyacinth, leaned against the doorframe, his lips curling up on one side into a crooked grin.

Sterling paused. Why was Beckett smiling?

Hyacinth narrowed her eyes on him, probably wondering the same thing.

"Fine. I'll do it." Beckett didn't take his gaze from Hyacinth. "Reckon it might be fun."

Hyacinth lifted her chin. "Fun? It will be the furthest thing from fun."

"Oh, darlin'," Beckett drawled. "Don't you worry your pretty little head. I'll make sure it's plenty of fun." Then he winked.

Sterling almost snorted, but then he caught Violet's gaze, filled with worry.

Before he could figure out what to say, Hyacinth was already responding. "I refuse to be connected to this—this—buffoon for any length of time."

"Buffoon?" Beckett lifted his hat, revealing more of the humor in his face. "What, are we back in the Middle Ages?"

"You go farther back than that to the barbaric Dark Ages." Hyacinth had a sharp tongue. Sterling had already known that. But she was proving to be even sharper than he'd realized.

Beckett didn't seem to mind her jabs. If anything, he was enjoying them, even gaining momentum from them. "Most women like how tough I am." He flexed one of his arms, showing off the ripples of his muscles against the tight fabric of his coat.

"I'm not like most women."

"That's for sure."

She sniffed, her eyes turning cold. "What's that supposed to mean?"

"It means you're a one-of-a-kind peacock."

"Peacock? I doubt you even know what a peacock is."

Beckett's grin had only widened over the course of the conversation. Was that the sign he was willing to go for the plan?

Sterling glanced between the two. "So you'll pretend to be a couple?"

"No," Hyacinth said.

"Yes." Beckett answered at the same time. "Course we will."

"We won't."

"Hyacinth." Violet reached for her sister's hands. "Please. Sometimes we have to do things we don't like in order to make ourselves stronger in the process."

Something sharp pricked Sterling's heart. What was Violet saying? That she'd agreed to marry him even though she didn't want to in order to make herself stronger?

The two sisters were quiet for a long moment, and Violet seemed to be silently pleading with Hyacinth to cooperate the same way she was. Was that all the marriage was for Violet? Cooperating with the plans in order to save them both from an uncertain future?

Sterling could feel the thrill from their recent kiss draining from him. Had he been the foolish one to allow himself to think Violet could want more from their relationship? What if the kiss had been more about convincing herself to marry him than being attracted to him?

"How long will I need to pretend to be engaged to…" Hyacinth paused, tossed a dark look at Beckett, then focused back on Violet. "To him."

Violet pressed her hand against her sister's cheek. "Just as long as it takes for us to figure things out and not a day longer."

Was that true for Violet too? Was she planning to stay married to him only for as long as it took to figure things out and not a day longer?

Sterling wanted to shake his head in protest and shout out that he couldn't do it, that it wouldn't be fair, that he wasn't strong enough to have her and then let her go.

But he bit back the words. As hard as it might be—maybe even the hardest thing he'd ever done—he intended to keep his word to Violet. Their marriage would only be temporary. When the time came to let her go, he would force himself to be brave enough to release her.

He had to follow through with his promise, even if it killed him to do so. Stiffening his shoulders, he crossed to the door. He had to leave now before either one of them changed their minds.

"Hey, baby," Beckett called from the hallway where he was standing watch by the front door. "Would you mind bringing me a cup of coffee?"

In the kitchen, Hyacinth looked up from where she was pouring herself a mug. Her eyes flashed with annoyance as she turned toward the hallway. "I'm not your *baby*."

"Course you are, darlin'."

Hyacinth expelled a taut breath before reaching for another mug and plopping it down on the stove. "I ought to dump vinegar in it."

"Go ahead," Beckett called, clearly hearing Hyacinth. "Then it will remind me of you—hot but full of sass."

Hyacinth just shook her head this time, probably not able to think of a comeback. Beckett was sharp-witted and sparred well with Hyacinth. The two had been exchanging insults for the past hour while they'd been waiting for the ranch hand to return with the reverend.

Part of Violet was entertained by the interchange. But another part of her didn't quite know what to think of the pretend engagement plan. If Hyacinth and Beckett couldn't get along in private, couldn't even stand to be in the same room as each other, how would they be able to prove to everyone they were engaged?

At least with Sterling, Violet was most definitely attracted to him.

She twisted her coffee mug around on the table in front of her. Yes, there was no doubt she was attracted to Sterling. She was so attracted she'd asked him for another kiss, even though she'd warned herself not to.

Heat infused her face at just the thought of how she'd practically begged him.

She lifted her cup and took a sip, hoping the steam from the coffee would mask any flush. Hyacinth hadn't asked her about the kiss yet, and Violet wasn't sure if she wanted to say anything.

Of course, Hyacinth was too busy with her frustration over Beckett to notice. Which was probably a good thing since Violet was confused about what to do with all the emotions bubbling inside her.

At Sterling's abrupt departure a short while ago, a whole host of doubts had come rushing back in—was she really ready, was she doing the right thing, was there another way out of her predicament, would she be safe with Sterling, would he ever be able to love her?

The questions had been clamoring, and she hadn't been able to answer a single one.

Sterling had come back inside not long ago and had gone upstairs to sleep for a short while. A part of her wanted to go up and talk to him again and discover what he was really feeling.

Maybe the two of them should have a pretend engagement like Hyacinth and Beckett. Why go to all the trouble of getting married if it wasn't necessary and especially if he didn't really want it and planned to annul their union at some point?

At a shout outside in the ranch yard, Violet placed her cup of coffee on the table. Hyacinth had finished pouring a mug for Beckett. In the process of carrying it toward the hallway door, she paused.

It was probably the ranch hand returning with the reverend.

A tremor rippled through Violet. Was she ready for this?

She closed her eyes and fought back a wave of panic. What was wrong with her? When she'd been getting dressed with Hyacinth earlier, she'd felt such anticipation putting on her best gown, taking extra care with her appearance, and trying to look her best.

While she'd waited in the parlor for Sterling to appear, she'd been excited, and yes, a little nervous. But mostly excited. And determined to follow through, to have courage, and to marry for love. Now that the moment had arrived, could she really go through with it?

Another shout came louder, followed by a gunshot.

Violet froze.

There wouldn't be gunshots if the reverend had arrived.

"Get down and away from windows." The urgent call came from Beckett.

Hyacinth hurriedly approached the table and placed the mug there.

Violet rose from her chair. Where should they go that would be safe?

Hyacinth passed Violet her crutch, all the while studying the layout of the kitchen and seeking a place to hide.

Another shot rang out.

"Come into the hallway, away from windows," Beckett called again, this time more urgently.

At the footsteps in the hallway upstairs, Violet guessed Sterling had heard the shot too.

Hyacinth took hold of Violet's arm. "Let's go."

Violet couldn't move fast with her crutch, but she crossed as quickly as she could to the hallway with Hyacinth. As they stepped into the corridor, Beckett had the front door open a crack and was peering outside.

Sterling thundered down the steps in his Sunday

best—a dark suit with a starched white dress shirt and a string tie. He was in the process of situating his hat and had a revolver out. His jaw was rigid and his eyes hard as he approached the door. "How many?"

Beckett shut the door and then locked it. "Six, maybe eight."

How would they ever fight six or eight men? Especially without someone getting hurt.

Violet's chest pinched tightly. She didn't want anyone suffering on account of her and Hyacinth, especially Sterling. But what could she do?

Should she step outside and try to negotiate with Claude's men? Or would that only put her and Hyacinth in more danger?

She shuffled forward a step.

The movement drew Sterling's sharp gaze. He held out a hand and cocked his head toward a short bureau that the family used for hats, gloves, handkerchiefs, and umbrellas. "Stop and get down low next to that."

His eyes warned her not to argue with him—not that she was prone to arguing the way Hyacinth was. Instead, she made her way to the bureau and lowered herself down the wall as Hyacinth did the same. When they were huddled side by side with the chest of drawers acting as a shield, only then did she allow herself a full breath.

Two more shots rang out. One pinged against the front door. The other shattered a parlor window, the glass crackling and tinkling as it fell to the floor.

Sterling and Beckett crouched together and talked in low tones for a minute before Beckett crawled into the parlor. Sterling started back up the stairs, taking them two at a time.

He paused halfway up and pinned Violet with a serious look. "Stay right there. And don't move until one of us says it's okay."

She nodded.

Hyacinth grasped Violet's hand and squeezed it. "I can't sit here and do nothing, Violet."

"We have to listen to Sterling."

"No," Hyacinth whispered back. "We have to figure this out on our own."

Violet wished they could. But wasn't that what had gotten them into the predicament to begin with? Mother had wanted to keep their affairs private. Instead of involving the law in Father's thefts in his places of employment, she'd paid his way out of the problems. And instead of seeking help for Father, Mother had just covered up the issues.

If they'd been more open to talking about their problems and asking for help, would Violet have felt more open to telling Sterling about her father's gambling rather than keeping it from him? Maybe if they hadn't been so embarrassed and isolated, they would have made more friends, had more support, and she wouldn't have had to turn to her ex-fiancé for help.

She had to do better in the future. She couldn't hide the problems, had to be more vulnerable, had to let others share the burdens. Because sometimes life's problems were too heavy to carry by oneself.

"Hold the shooting!" came Sterling's shout from upstairs. "No more shooting!"

His tone held a strange desperation that sent Violet's heart thumping with a strange fear. Something was wrong.

She wanted to get up and go to him, but she'd promised him she would wait by the chest of drawers.

A voice boomed from the yard outside the house. "If you want him to live, then hand over the women."

Him?

"If you don't do it," said the booming voice, "then you'll force me to get rid of this worthless, sniveling son of a gun myself."

Violet sat up at the same time that Hyacinth did. Was the worthless, sniveling son of a gun their father? Who else could it be?

Hyacinth started to climb to her feet, her features set with determination. What was she planning to do? Run outside and give herself over in exchange for their father?

Violet pulled her back down. "No, Hyacinth. We have to think."

Sterling couldn't claim her as his wife yet, but could

he tell Claude's men that she was his fiancée the way they'd planned to introduce Hyacinth as Beckett's fiancée?

"I'm marrying Violet today, this morning." Sterling's shout came from the upstairs room at the front of the house. He was clearly thinking the same way she was. "And Hyacinth is engaged to be married to my foreman, Beckett Thorpe."

"If they're not lawfully yours, then they still belong to Claude." The spokesperson for Claude's posse was obviously not willing to show any mercy. "Marvin shook on a deal, which in this country is as good as done."

"The reverend is on his way," Sterling responded.

A moment of silence ensued. Were Claude's men trying to decide what to do?

Violet closed her eyes. The situation had no solution. From the way it sounded, Claude's men had been instructed to bring in her and Hyacinth or kill Father.

She couldn't sit back and let them murder Father. But she still wasn't willing to hand herself or Hyacinth over...

Could Father pay off the debt in increments? But where would he be able to find work? And even if someone in the area were willing to hire him, would he gamble the money right away and then cause even more problems?

Even if so, she had to suggest the option. Claude could have Father work for him in some capacity until he earned back what he owed.

Yes, that's what had to happen. Father had to make himself a slave to Claude—if necessary—until the debt was paid. Surely Father would be willing to do that if the option were presented to him. She had to believe that some part of him still cared about her and Hyacinth enough that he would do the right thing.

With determination stiffening her spine, she rose, fixed her crutch under her arm, and started down the hallway toward the front door.

Sterling wouldn't like her getting involved in the negotiations. But she needed to offer the idea as an option.

"Where are you going?" Hyacinth whispered behind her, already on her feet.

Violet tried to pick up her halting pace, which wasn't easy with the crutch. But she didn't want Hyacinth close enough to impede her efforts and was at the front door within seconds.

"You can't go out—"

Violet swung the door wide, then stepped outside onto the porch.

There, in the middle of the ranch yard, stood a burly man with a scarred face, her father positioned in front of him like a shield. Her father's hatless head hung low, but she could see enough to tell that his face was bruised and battered, both eyes swollen nearly shut, his lips cut and bleeding, and a rope with a slip knot already dangling from his chafed neck. His clothing was stained and rumpled, as if he'd been wearing the same outfit for days.

Violet couldn't hold back her gasp at the sad state her father was in, and tears quickly sprang to her eyes.

The fellow holding her father shifted his attention to her. "You the daughter?"

From the window above, Sterling said something, and Beckett called out too. But she was too focused on her father and his dismal condition to listen.

Her father lifted his head in her direction. He barely had the strength to look at her, but somehow his gaze connected with hers. "I'm sorry."

"Come on out here, darlin'." The scar-faced man beckoned to Violet. "It's you and your sister for him."

As angry as she was with her father for all his mistakes and the ways he'd failed to protect their family, she couldn't stand back and watch these men hang him in the closest tree.

Behind her, Hyacinth stood stiffly, probably just as appalled by the sight of their father.

"We can make this nice and easy," the man said. "No sense in dragging this out more."

The fellow was right about that. Violet had to bring an end to the problems today. She couldn't run away from them any longer, no matter how much she wanted to.

Sterling's pulse thundered with dread, and he couldn't get his feet to work fast enough to carry him down the stairs.

"Violet!" Fear strangled his voice. "No, Violet!"

He was too late to keep her from going outside, but he had to prevent her from doing something foolish, like handing herself over to Claude's men in exchange for her father.

From midway down the stairs, he could see Beckett had already moved from the parlor to the front door.

"Get them back inside," Sterling roared as Beckett lunged outside. "Get them in now!"

Sterling stumbled down the last of the steps, and as he raced to the door, Beckett backed inside with Hyacinth struggling in his arms.

"Let go of me, you oaf!" Her eyes flashed murder at Beckett. "I'm not leaving Violet out there by herself."

Sterling pushed past the two, only one thought filling

his head. He had to get to Violet. That was all that mattered.

Violet had crossed the porch to the front step as if she had every intention of walking over and taking her father's place.

He bounded after her. "Violet, stop!"

A gunshot rang out, and an instant later, a bullet whizzed past him. It was far enough away that whoever had fired it had likely done so as a warning, perhaps to stop him. The men might be willing to hang Violet's father, but they wouldn't dare kill Sterling. They'd never get away with it, and they obviously knew it.

Warning or not, he didn't halt until he reached Violet. He threw himself in front of her, shoving her behind his body. "No!" The word ripped from him and contained all the anguish that had been racing through him since the moment he'd realized she'd gone outside.

Thankfully, she was more compliant than Hyacinth and didn't try to break free from his grip on her.

His breathing was labored, and his heart pounded against his ribs. But he took a deep breath because he had Violet in a safe place, and he didn't plan to let her go.

At the same time, he knew he couldn't let Mr. Berkley die, especially with Violet and Hyacinth watching. Her father deserved the consequences for gambling away his family's money and safety. But he didn't deserve to hang for it.

With one hand pinning Violet behind him, he aimed his gun toward the man holding Mr. Berkley. He was a giant of a man with a red face that had a wide scar across one cheek. He held himself with an authority that marked him as the leader. "Tell your men not to shoot again."

In the distance by the barns, several of Sterling's ranch hands had their guns trained upon Claude's men, who were spread out and had taken cover behind other outbuildings, feeding troughs, and watering barrels. It was clear the men had come with the intention of fighting, and Sterling didn't want to chance any bullets coming anywhere near Violet.

"If you want a stand-down," the big fellow responded, "then hand over the women."

"That won't happen."

"Then you leave us with no choice but to bring about justice for this man's swindling."

Violet shifted, her head poking out from behind Sterling. "Could my father work off his debt at the saloon?"

Sterling pushed her back out of sight. She was raising a valid question, but he doubted Claude, or any saloon owner, would be willing to set a precedent of hiring the men who racked up debt with them.

On the other hand...

Sterling's mind sped with a new possibility. "How much money does Mr. Berkley owe the Red Cap?"

Claude's henchman shook Mr. Berkley. "Tell everyone what you owe Claude."

Shoulders slumped and head bent, Violet's father didn't look up.

"Tell them." The fellow's voice rose with anger.

Violet's dad mumbled something.

"Louder." Claude's man slapped Mr. Berkley across the head.

"Two thousand dollars." This time Mr. Berkley's voice was clear but also filled with self-loathing.

Behind him, Violet released a breath that contained her defeat. Two thousand was more than an average man made in a year by far. In fact, it would take most ranch hands five years to earn that amount.

But Sterling had close to that amount—the money he'd earned and saved for years. When he'd been engaged to Violet, he'd planned to use it to build their house as well as purchase all the furnishings they would need for every room.

The problem was that he didn't have exactly two thousand. He was short by a few hundred.

He turned his sights to the herd grazing on the bales of alfalfa the ranch hands had fed them this morning. He could sell off some of the steers to make up the difference.

But with the blackleg that had run through his herd, he'd already lost too many. While he was beginning to feel confident that the vaccination Thatcher had administered would stop the spread to more livestock, Sterling wasn't entirely sure yet. In addition, he still had the rest of the winter to get through, with the usual losses that came when cattle got sick, got lost, or froze to death.

Already, his dad would be disappointed to learn of the problems. If Sterling sold some off and depleted the herd further, Dad would be really upset, would maybe even give the ranch administration job to one of his other sons—probably Coleman, who had always been the favorite.

Exactly how many cattle would it take to make up the difference with the two thousand dollars?

Sterling swiftly began calculating. Their newest breed was going for a premium price because the Durham provided a better cut of meat. If he could get twenty dollars a head, he would need to sell at least a dozen, if not more. He would probably find a market for the beef up in Leadville. But getting the steers all the way up to the high mountain town would be difficult with the recent snow.

Sterling could feel all eyes upon him—his ranch hands' as well as Claude's men's. Even Violet and Hyacinth and Beckett were watching him. They were waiting for him to come up with a solution.

Dad would likely remind Sterling that if he'd gone to school and bettered himself, he would have had more skills and a greater ability to handle problems and issues that arose.

Sterling's muscles tightened. It was too late to compare himself to his brothers. And he didn't have time at the moment to worry about his dad getting angry. No, he had to act quickly if he wanted to save Mr. Berkley.

"Release Mr. Berkley to me," Sterling said as his mind continued to scramble to formulate a plan.

Behind him, Violet grew motionless.

The fellow holding Violet's dad released a scoff. "And why would I do that?"

"He'll work off his debt to me for the next five years as a ranch hand."

"Claude won't wait five years for Marvin to pay off his debt in slow increments."

"He won't need to wait five years."

The henchman shook his head. "Claude won't wait even a year. He knows fellows like this head right back to the gambling table the minute they get a penny."

"He won't get a penny." Sterling spoke firmly. "All he'll get is room and board. His earnings will go right to me."

Claude's man finally raised his brow.

"To pay me back."

Violet gasped and started to struggle against his hold. "No, Sterling."

"Yes." He strained to keep her behind him. "I'll give Claude the two thousand dollars, and then Mr. Berkley will work for me until he clears his debt."

Violet's father raised his head and peered at Sterling through his bruised and swollen eyes.

"Will you agree to the plan, Mr. Berkley?" Sterling guessed the middle-aged man probably didn't know the first thing about being a ranch hand and would need a lot of training before he was proficient enough to earn his keep. But there were plenty of easy but mundane chores around the ranch that he could do while he learned.

"I'll do anything." Mr. Berkley spoke in a wobbly voice, that of a broken man who knew he'd come close to dying and was getting a second chance.

"You'll sign an agreement that says you'll work for me for five years."

"Yes. No question about it."

"Good. Then we have a deal." Sterling didn't know all the lawyer language, but he'd watched his father work and talk long enough to know a little bit. He could write up a simple contract and make sure it was legal and bound Mr. Berkley to Noble Ranch until the debt was repaid.

Claude's henchman didn't immediately respond.

Sterling's gut churned. He might be ruining himself with such a bargain. It was possible his dad would never deed him the ranch now. Instead, he'd be angry and call Sterling a fool.

Maybe he was a fool. But he'd rather save Violet's

father for her sake than have the best, biggest, and most profitable ranch in Colorado. She was more important to him than success. She was more important to him than anything. And this was his start in showing her that.

"I'll ride to the bank this morning," Sterling continued, "and bring Claude all but three hundred of the money." Sterling had some hidden in a safe in the house, and the rest was locked away at the bank.

The henchman loosened his hold on Mr. Berkley. "Claude won't accept anything less than two thousand."

"It'll take me a few more days to get the last of the three hundred. But you can tell Claude I'm good for it."

He could feel Violet beginning to tremble behind him. What did she think of his plan? She hadn't protested yet. Probably because she knew, like he did, that it was the only option.

Claude's man began to drag Mr. Berkley back to his horse.

"Leave him here." Sterling waved his gun. He hadn't holstered it yet and wouldn't until the men were gone.

The henchman again pulled Mr. Berkley in front of his body, then glowered at Sterling. "If I return to Claude empty-handed, I'll be the dead man."

Sterling didn't want to chance Mr. Berkley going anywhere near Claude again. The best thing was for him to remain at the ranch. Violet and Hyacinth could tend to his wounds, then Beckett could get him settled into the bunkhouse.

"Mr. Berkley is staying." Sterling spoke in his most authoritative tone. "I'll go back to town with you in his place."

The fellow's eyes widened.

"You can go with me to the bank," Sterling offered. "Then you can take me directly to Claude after that."

The henchman hesitated for a few more long seconds. Then he shoved Violet's father away from him. The move was unexpected, and Mr. Berkley stumbled forward, then fell to his knees in the matted grass.

Violet gave a soft cry of distress and tried to break free. This time, Sterling let her go. She shuffled past him, then down the steps and across the grass.

In the next instant, Hyacinth was running toward Mr. Berkley too.

Beckett stepped beside Sterling, his expression grave. "You're giving away all of your savings?"

"Yes."

"And you're selling off a dozen steers for the rest."

Sterling nodded.

Beckett blew out an exasperated breath. "I hope she's worth it, boss. I really do. Because you're giving up everything for her."

Sterling knew he'd done the right thing. But a sick feeling settled in his stomach—the feeling that he hadn't given up everything yet and the worst was yet to come.

Sterling placed the stack of cash in front of Claude where he sat alone at the gaming table.

In the middle of taking a puff on a limp cigar, the tiny man paused and eyed the cash. With a head of thinning red hair, a narrow mustache, pasty white skin, and a slight frame, the saloon owner was not the man Sterling had expected.

The gaming room was also not what Sterling had expected. It was filled with morning sunshine, the several tables with chairs were immaculate, the floor was spotless, and the air held a fresh lemon scent.

Several of Claude's men stood near the door, including the scar-faced one who had been in charge of the operation and apparently went by the name of Tiny.

"What's this?" Claude's voice came out surprisingly deep and coarse for a man of his small stature.

Tiny cleared his throat. "It's the payment for Mr.

Berkley's debt. Or at least, most of it."

"I'll have the final three hundred to you in a few days." Sterling pushed the cash closer to Claude. "Just as soon as I get back from selling some of my beef."

Claude sized up Sterling, his hard eyes taking him in from his hat down to his boots. He was still wearing his Sunday best in preparation for the wedding that hadn't taken place.

A wedding.

The whole ride into town with Claude's men and all the while at the bank, Sterling hadn't been able to contain the disappointment that was building inside him. He'd been so close again to getting married to Violet. He'd washed up, shaved, and changed into a suit in preparation. But would they need a wedding now?

The truth was, now that Sterling was paying off the debt, Claude would have no more reason to come after Violet and Hyacinth. They would be free to come and go as they pleased without any worry about being turned into dancehall girls.

"Did you count it?" Claude asked another fellow, one wearing a suit and glasses, his hair slicked back. He looked like he might be a bookkeeper rather than a henchman.

The fellow nodded. "It's seventeen hundred."

Claude flipped through the bills, tapped a finger on the top of the stack, then nodded at it.

The bookkeeper stepped up to the table, gathered the money, and slipped it into a leather satchel.

Claude sat back and peered at Sterling again. "I'll expect the final payment in no more than a week."

"I appreciate it." The fellow seemed fair enough. He'd likely given Mr. Berkley plenty of chances to pay off his debt. Even so, the world of gambling was a dangerous one, and Sterling would be relieved when the whole ordeal was over.

Sterling turned to go. He had a lot of work ahead of him over the next few days if he hoped to pay Claude the final three hundred.

Claude's voice stopped him. "I don't know why you helped Mr. Berkley. But I hope you don't regret it."

Sterling glanced at the saloon owner, reclining in his chair at the table. "I don't."

"You should know, that man will be back. Gamblers like him can never stay away."

Sterling supposed the gaming table had a strong pull on some people. But Mr. Berkley wouldn't have a dime to spend in five years. If the pull of the gaming table wasn't broken in five years, then Sterling didn't know what could ever break it.

Claude took a puff on his cigar and eyed Sterling. "You won't be able to bail him out forever."

Sterling hoped Mr. Berkley had also learned a lesson through his brush with death. Whatever the case, Sterling intended to use Beckett to toughen the man up and make an honest worker out of him. The ranch, the work, the long days in the saddle would be hard on a fellow who was accustomed to being in an office. But Sterling had faith Beckett would be able to reform Mr. Berkley.

"I'll see you in a few days." Sterling didn't wait for Claude to say anything else and instead walked out of the saloon, got on his horse, and started back to the ranch.

He was in a hurry to return and urged his horse out of town at a gallop. All the while he rode, his mind kept pace. Would the reverend be there waiting? And if he was, what would they do about it?

As much as he wanted to push Violet forward with the wedding before she had a chance to change her mind and run away, a part of him knew he needed to consider abandoning the plans and sending the reverend home. He no longer had a valid reason for insisting on the marriage.

But strangely, his entire being was opposed to the prospect of cancelling the ceremony. The truth was, he wanted Violet any way he could have her, even if that meant they lived in a contrived marriage that was in name only.

Did that make him pathetic? Maybe. But he was desperate enough that he would do anything. If she was still willing, even though she no longer needed to go through with the wedding, that would be a good sign, wouldn't it?

Even as he made excuses, they echoed with a familiar ring…because they were the same excuses he'd made before the first wedding, when he'd tried to tell himself it didn't matter if she loved him less, if she wasn't as invested in their marriage, if she didn't want him as much.

He'd insisted his love could carry them both. But it hadn't.

As he finally rode underneath the front gate of wrought iron with the Noble Ranch sign hanging overhead, he let himself take a full breath. Some of the ranch hands were fixing fences. A few others were working on a leaky spot on one of the barn roofs. The cattle were fenced in where they should be. And everything appeared to be back to normal.

The visit by Claude's men could have ended much differently, with more destruction, injuries, and even loss of lives. Sterling had to count his blessings, especially that the women were safe and unharmed.

As he drew closer, he spotted a horse tied to a rail next to the barn—an old mare that didn't belong to any of his ranch hands.

His heart gave an extra thud. The mare had to belong to the reverend.

Sterling didn't waste time taking his horse to the barn and instead veered directly toward the house. At Sterling's approach, Beckett stepped outside and headed down the steps.

"Well?" Beckett asked, his brow furrowed with worry.

"Claude agreed to the deal and gave me until the end of the week to get him the final payment."

Beckett's expression remained grim. "You're gonna sell a dozen Durfords?"

Doing so would nearly deplete their stock of the prized cattle. Of course, they'd already had their breeding season earlier in the fall and had numerous cows that would deliver more Durfords in the spring...if all went well and no more died.

But still, selling the cattle wasn't going to make the ranch more successful. It wasn't a good business strategy. In fact, it was terrible. But he had to do it anyway.

Sterling dismounted and tossed the lead line over the porch railing. "Have the fellows separate out the beeves that are the thickest."

"When we aiming to leave?"

"I'm going." Sterling halted. "I need you here to keep an eye on things, make sure Claude doesn't change his mind."

Beckett twisted the piece of hay in his mouth. He didn't protest, almost as if he'd expected the instructions.

Sterling straightened his tie.

Beckett narrowed his eyes. "Reckon we can send the preacher on home now that we don't need him."

Sterling didn't want to argue with Beckett about his relationship with Violet right here and now. "I'll see what

Violet wants to do."

If her kisses from the past day were any indication, then her passion and her desire for him had grown. He hadn't imagined it. There was something different between them. At least, he wanted to believe they were different this time.

Sterling started up the steps.

Beckett followed more slowly, probably wanting to chastise him to be careful but holding himself back.

As Sterling entered, he listened for the sound of voices.

"In the kitchen." Beckett nodded down the hallway.

Sterling hadn't been sure what to expect when he entered the kitchen, but he was unprepared for Mr. Berkley to be weeping openly at the table. Hyacinth was gently washing the abrasions on his neck, and Violet was sitting beside him, holding his hand. Reverend Livingston was also seated beside him, speaking with him.

At Sterling's appearance, Mr. Berkley lifted a handkerchief to his nose and blew noisily, trying to compose himself. He'd taken quite a beating from Claude's men, probably had bruises and cuts in places they couldn't see, maybe even broken ribs. But he was alive, and he would eventually heal. Hopefully he could find healing both outwardly and inwardly.

Violet released her father's hand, stood, and crossed to Sterling, her eyes bright with unshed tears. She started to reach for him as if she might throw herself against him in a hug, but she stopped short and clasped her hands together.

"Oh, Sterling," she whispered with a tremulous smile. "I don't know how I can thank you."

She was just as beautiful in her green gown now as she'd been at dawn. The vibrant color made her eyes all the greener, like a mountain forest, and he wanted to wander in them all day. The color also made her pale skin look like silk so that he wished he could skim his hands over it.

Sterling could feel everyone staring at them, and a flush began to work its way around his collar. He needed to have an important conversation with Violet about their future and what to do with the reverend now that he was at the house, but he didn't want to have an audience. "Let's talk in the hallway."

They stepped out of the kitchen, and he closed the door for privacy. Beckett was nowhere to be seen, had probably gone out to the field to start separating the cattle to sell.

"You don't have to thank me, Violet." He fidgeted with his tie again.

"You're amazing." Her voice held reverence, and she clasped his hands and brought them down between them.

The clanging in his head, which had been getting louder, turned suddenly silent. Maybe everything would be all right. Maybe he was worrying for nothing.

"You didn't have to do any of what you did," she continued, a soft smile playing at her lips.

Those pretty, kissable lips that tasted like everything good in the world. Holy sweet heavens, what he wouldn't do or give to kiss those lips again. But he couldn't at this moment. He needed to focus on the conversation they needed to have about their future.

"I'm in debt to you." Her voice was earnest.

He didn't want to think about her being in debt to him. That hadn't been his intention in helping her father. "Your father will have to work it off."

"But you have no guarantee he will."

Sterling curled his fingers around hers more firmly. That was true. It was also true he would have to start saving all over again, which would take years. That meant he wouldn't have the means to build a house for a wife anytime soon…a house for Violet?

"I'm hopeful, though," Violet continued. "Father seems truly sorrowful. After all that's happened, I think he understands the mistakes he's made."

"That's a start."

She squeezed Sterling's hands.

He loved her closeness and wanted to throw away all caution and just draw her into his arms.

"I'll never be able to thank you enough." Her eyes turned glassy again. "I owe you everything for saving me and Hyacinth and my father."

Debt. Owe everything.

A strange sick feeling wafted through him. If he pressured her to go through with marrying him today, she would do it. Out of obligation. To thank him. Because she wanted to pay him back for the debt she felt she owed him.

But he couldn't let her marry him for those reasons. He didn't want her to feel beholden to him for anything—not for giving her a job, not for helping her and Hyacinth, and not for paying her father's gambling debt.

He wouldn't do that, even if she was agreeable. If he did, he'd always feel like she'd gone through with marrying him because she'd had to, not because she'd wanted to. He refused to take advantage of her that way.

"It was the right thing to do, Violet." He let go of her hands and took a step back, needing some distance. "The other right thing is to release you from any commitment to me."

Her brows rose, as if his statement was the last thing she'd expected to hear.

Maybe after how much he'd pressured her to marry him the first time, it was unexpected. Maybe she'd thought he'd pressure her today, especially with the reverend visiting. But he was different now—or at least, he wanted to be a changed man who could love authentically and sacrificially.

Part of learning to love her in a real way was giving her up—giving up any right to her or a future with her.

She glanced down at her fancy gown, her expression turning shy. "I don't mind, Sterling. If you still want to go through with the wedding today, we can, since the reverend is here and we're ready. But only if you want to. It's all right if you don't. I'm not expecting you to…"

Was she rambling because she was nervous?

He needed to put her at ease and assure her that he cared but also that he wouldn't expect anything from her. Could he be honest with her? He wanted her to know how he felt but also that he was giving her the freedom to choose her own future.

He cleared his throat and forced himself to speak. "I need to be honest with you, Violet."

She didn't lift her gaze, was instead fiddling with the hem of her sleeve.

"I must admit, I still love you."

At his declaration, her gaze shot up to his. Her beautiful green eyes held something he couldn't name. Was it hope?

Whatever the case, he had to keep going. "Yes, I can't deny that I love you and always have. But this time, I want to love you better. Which means I can't manipulate you into marrying me because you feel you owe me something. I have to wait and be patient for you to be ready."

A part of him wanted her to interrupt and tell him she was ready, that she loved him too, that she was finally ready to be with him.

She opened her lips to say something, then stalled before closing her mouth and dropping her gaze once more.

A heavy boulder fell to the bottom of his stomach. He had the overwhelming urge to grab her hands, plead with her, and promise that everything would be okay. But doing so would be about him and his needs and wouldn't be about her.

"Even if you're never ready, that's okay." The words were difficult to get out, but once they were, he knew he'd taken a step forward in his journey of learning to love better. He'd given her up, which was harder than giving up his savings. "And you and Hyacinth can work here at the ranch as long as you want. There's plenty to do, and I'm sure Jo-Jo will appreciate the help in the spring when she returns."

"Thank you." Violet stared at her hands.

He pushed himself back another step toward the door. "I'll be gone a few days selling some cattle. While I'm away, Beckett will make sure you're safe and that your father does what he needs to."

"Okay." Her voice was quiet.

She was pulling away from him. He could see it in the way she held herself and in her expression. Was she frightened by his declaration of love? Was she relieved that he wasn't pressuring her into marriage again? What emotions were running through her?

He wished she would open up and tell him how she was feeling instead of closing herself off like she had last time.

It was obvious she still wasn't ready to marry him, perhaps still didn't love him.

Choking down his frustration, he spun on his heels and started toward the front door. It was best for him to go. Hopefully the time apart would give him a fresh perspective so that when he came back, he could love her freely without any reciprocation. If that's what he would have to do for the rest of his life, could he? Could he be around her but never have her?

He blew out a tight breath, then exited through the front door without a glance back.

# 21

She was free.

Violet paused in her newest redecorating project in the dining room. She stared unseeingly out the window at the ranch yard bathed in morning light.

She might be free, but she felt more burdened than ever before.

"What's wrong?" Hyacinth paused over the new plum-colored drapery she was sewing at the dining room table, which was currently filled with the supplies they'd been using to transform the room from simple into elegant.

Over the past four days since the confrontation with Claude's men and Sterling's paying off Father's debt, she and Hyacinth had kept themselves busy with thoroughly cleaning and organizing the house. Of course, with just the two of them there, they'd finished cleaning and organizing fairly quickly.

That was fine with Violet. She'd much rather focus on decorating than on cleaning. Since they'd already completed overhauling the parlor, they'd started on the dining room. They were making new drapes from elegant material they'd located in the attic.

Violet was in the process of repainting the candelabras a gilded gold with paint from among the decorating supplies that had been left at their house in Breckenridge. Beckett had kindly taken some of the ranch hands into town to help move out the rest of their belongings, including the boxes of Violet's interior designing materials. The men had loaded the items into a wagon and brought them out to the ranch.

She and Hyacinth didn't have a lot of belongings left, certainly not anything of value. But Violet had been relieved to save a few trunks of her mother's possessions, a crate of books, and more of their clothing as well as sentimental items.

The mementos brought back happy memories of decorating with her mother and sister, reminding Violet that not all of her childhood had been difficult. They also reminded her that she couldn't keep getting stuck in her past and in all that had happened. She had to move on.

But she hadn't.

With an exasperated sigh, she set her paintbrush down and reclined in the dining room chair, her sprained foot elevated on the chair across from her.

Hyacinth was still watching her with a narrowed gaze. "Go talk to him."

Sterling had arrived home late last night after she and Hyacinth had gone to bed. Violet had heard him come in and tread lightly up the stairway. She'd wanted to get up and greet him, had been nearly breathless with the need to see him. But she'd lain in bed stiffly, letting the war rage inside her—a war that was still going on this morning...and that she was losing.

"I can't talk to him." She wanted to and had even gone down to the kitchen before dawn, hoping to catch him there. But when he'd risen, he'd headed out the front door without a word. "He doesn't want to see me."

It was Hyacinth's turn to release an exasperated breath. "He told you he loves you."

Even though she and Sterling had closed the door for their conversation in the hallway that day he'd left to sell the steers, apparently Hyacinth had heard every word they'd spoken.

Violet hadn't been upset at her sister's eavesdropping because, as usual, it had saved her from having to explain why she and Sterling weren't getting married.

It also meant that Hyacinth knew every detail of how Sterling felt about Violet—how he didn't want to pressure her into marriage, how he wanted to be patient.

"You can't wait for him to come talk to you this time." Hyacinth picked up her needle and material. "No, he made it clear how he feels and what his position is. Now it's your turn to go to him and tell him how you feel."

"But how do I feel?" The question was silly. She knew. Because the fact was, she loved Sterling more than anything or anyone. She had no doubt about her love, probably never had, had just let her fears influence her.

Hyacinth snorted, clearly recognizing the same thing. "Knowing Sterling, he won't approach you about it again."

A twinge of alarm rang inside Violet. "He won't?"

"Of course not. He's a proud and stubborn man. He played his game pieces, and now the next move is up to you."

Hyacinth was right. It was her move now. But her sister was wrong in thinking she and Sterling were playing a game. This thing between her and Sterling was no game. It was very real. If only she hadn't gotten scared that morning in the hallway. When he'd told her he loved her. If only she'd responded to him then. She'd wanted to. But that same feeling she'd had on her wedding day had come back—the feeling that love wasn't reliable and stability wasn't possible.

But of course, Sterling had proven he was reliable and stable time and time again. He'd even wanted to show her real love by sacrificing for her—using all his savings and then some to save her father's life. Through it all, he hadn't asked her for anything in return. In fact, he'd walked away from her to prove to them both that he didn't want anything back, that he was forfeiting everything freely.

What kind of man would do that? Not very many. But he'd done it for her. He'd shown her that his love was unselfish and that he wasn't like her father.

Now it was up to her to take the next step and accept him and his love. Even though she was still scared, she had to do her part.

"I should have told him I loved him when he said it to me."

Hyacinth was back to her quick but neat stitching. "Regardless of your failings—"

"Failings?"

"Yes, that man laid his heart out to you, and you basically rejected him again."

The alarm inside Violet swelled into panic. "Do you really think I rejected him again?"

"He might feel that way. Maybe that's why he's steering clear of you since he got home. Maybe he's hurt and not sure how to act around you."

"Oh no." Violet pushed back from the table, her stomach churning. "What should I do?"

"You have to decide if you want him enough to face your fears."

"I do want him enough to face my fears, but how can

I do that?"

Hyacinth stitched quietly for a moment, then halted and looked up at Violet with a gleam in her eyes.

"Do you really want to show him that you love him and want to marry him?"

Violet swallowed any doubts lingering inside. "Yes."

Hyacinth placed her sewing on the table and stood with a smile. "I have an idea. A really big idea."

"I will take all the help I can get."

"I realize that." Hyacinth spoke wryly. "We need a foolproof plan that will make it impossible for you to run away from him, and force you to finally face your fears."

"Will your plan do that?"

Hyacinth's grin widened. "I do believe it will."

He missed Violet.

From the inside of the barn, Sterling glanced through the open door toward the house again. He wanted to go inside and just look at her. Take a quick peek. That's all.

But during the past few days that he'd been gone, he'd tried to strengthen his resolve to wait for her to be ready for him. And if he started spending time with her, even just to look at her, he'd lose his determination.

Exhaling a breath of frustration at himself, he stood next to Thatcher as the veterinarian doctored an abscess on the leg of one of the steers. It wasn't blackleg. That was the good news. But Thatcher wasn't sure what was causing the inflammation among several of the steers.

The problems would never end on a cattle ranch like theirs. It was just part of life, and he had to accept the successes as well as the setbacks because there would always be both.

He was learning a lot through it all. As much as he wanted to prove to his dad that he wasn't a failure for not going away to college, maybe he had to stop worrying about what his dad thought. Maybe his top priority had to be people. Ultimately, loving people well was more important than success. At least, he wanted that to be more important to him.

Sterling knew his dad might not understand his choice to sell the cattle, might be disappointed in him, might even let someone else manage the ranch in his stead. But that was okay. As long as Sterling could be proud of himself for his integrity, then he could live with his father's decision.

"That ought to do it." Thatcher finished wrapping a bandage around the oozing wound, then straightened.

"Thank you." Sterling tried to fix his attention back on the situation at hand. "I owe you a great deal of thanks for all you've done for me and the ranch."

Thatcher began to tuck his supplies back into the big brown leather satchel that he used for carrying supplies. "I'm happy to do it."

"If you ever need a favor, you know where to come."

Thatcher tossed him a grin. "I appreciate that, Sterling. You're a good man."

"You are too. Still no sign of your mail-order bride?"

Thatcher's smile faded, replaced by loneliness. "No, I'm afraid not. And from what I'm hearing, the travel from the Front Range up to the high country has pretty much stopped."

"So does that mean you'll have to wait until spring now for her arrival?"

"It looks that way." Thatcher picked up his satchel, his shoulders already slumped.

Sterling didn't want to think about living alone the way Thatcher did.

His gaze again slid out the barn door and to the house. Even though he couldn't have Violet right now, at least she was on the ranch nearby.

Now that the problems were gone and she no longer needed him in the same way, would she be ready to move on? Or at the very least move on from him?

With her father living on the ranch, he hoped she would stay. According to Beckett's report this morning, Mr. Berkley wasn't adjusting well to ranch life. He was soft, weak, and pampered. But thankfully he seemed determined to keep going, even though the work was hard for him.

At the moment, the fellow had nowhere else to go, no one else to turn to, and no other way to survive the coming winter. The ranch was probably the best place for him, since town and the gaming tables weren't within easy reach. The abstinence would hopefully help his cravings for gambling to eventually diminish.

As Sterling stepped out of the barn, a shout from

across the fields to the west caught his attention. He tipped up the brim of his hat and located a lone figure galloping across the soggy pasture. The snow from the previous week was now mostly gone, leaving only puddles behind.

The lanky but muscular body with the slouched shoulders belonged to Beckett. What was he doing out in the foothills when he'd said he had to run to town for an errand?

Sterling watched the foreman's approach, his body tensing. There weren't more problems with Claude, were there?

Sterling had stopped by Red Cap Saloon last night on his way home and delivered the final three hundred dollars to Claude himself. The saloon owner had shaken his hand, told him the deal was done, and wished him good luck. Surely the fellow wouldn't go back on his word.

"Saddle your horse," Beckett called when he was finally in shouting distance.

Saddle his horse? Sterling's pulse pounded harder. "What for?"

"It's the women."

Sterling didn't have to be told twice when it came to the women, to Violet. Without even a farewell to the veterinarian, Sterling took off at a jog toward the horse barn. He saddled his horse in record time and was leading his gelding out into the ranch yard when Beckett reined in near the barn.

From all appearances, Beckett didn't seem hurt or anxious.

"Are the women okay?" Sterling began to mount his horse.

"They're fine." Beckett's tone contained a note of irritation.

"They're not hurt?"

"Nope."

Sterling allowed himself a full breath—the first since seeing his foreman approaching. "Then what's wrong?"

Beckett spat out the piece of hay he'd been chewing, then his jaw flexed with his displeasure. "They went back out to the cabin."

Sterling's whole body ceased functioning, and he could only stare at his foreman.

"Yep. You heard me right."

Sterling scrambled to find a reason why they would do such a thing. Had someone threatened them again? Or was Violet running away from him?

He didn't even want to think about the second option. Couldn't bear the prospect that she wanted to get away from him, that maybe he'd scared her off by telling her of his love the other day.

"Did they say why they went?" And for that matter, with her ankle still not healed, how had she gotten there?

With the snowmelt of the past few days, there was the chance she'd ridden a horse for most of the distance and maybe only had to ski the last quarter of a mile. It would have been hard for her, but it was possible. Or maybe Hyacinth had taken the sled and pulled her the last portion.

"We need to get there as quickly as possible." Beckett didn't answer his question but instead shifted his horse back around, already nudging it into a trot.

Sterling did the same, and in no time, the two of them were racing across the field. The cold breeze hit Sterling's face, and the mud flew up around him, urging him faster. They rode hard for a short while until they reached the higher elevation, where the terrain was slippery and wet, forcing them to slow their pace.

When they finally reached the pastureland, Sterling nudged his horse beside Beckett's. "Do you know why they ran away out here again?" Sterling wasn't sure he wanted to know the answer and stiffened his shoulders to brace himself for the worst—that Violet didn't want to be near him.

Beckett glanced at him sideways. "I told them I wouldn't tell you."

"Shoot, Beckett." Sterling shook his head curtly, the frustration pooling inside. "Don't do this to me."

Beckett shrugged. "They're fine, though. I can tell you that."

"How'd they get up here?"

"Horses for most of the way. Then the skis and sled the last of the distance."

Just like he'd thought. "Why'd they come to you and not to me?"

"Reckon it's because I'm better-looking."

Sterling wasn't in the mood for joking, and he urged his horse faster, pulling ahead of Beckett. He didn't know what he'd say to Violet when he got to the cabin. But he had to say something to reassure her that they could get along together on the ranch just fine. He'd let her know he wasn't planning to restart their relationship and would give her as much distance and time as she needed. He thought he'd already made that clear, but apparently not enough.

Whatever the case was, he didn't want her running off to the cabin every time she felt like she needed to get away.

At the top of the next incline, he wasn't surprised to see two horses tied up to a tree. But he was surprised to discover one of the horses didn't belong to the Noble Ranch. The creature looked familiar, but he couldn't place where he'd seen it before.

He and Beckett dismounted, tied up their horses, then donned the skis that Beckett had left there for them. Once again, Beckett refused to say anything about the horse and skis, insisting that Sterling would discover the answers soon enough.

Sterling was a better skier than Beckett and left him behind in his haste to reach the cabin. Within five minutes, the log structure came into view in the forested nook near the creek. Smoke rose from the chimney, which thankfully meant this time the women had been able to start a fire. Or maybe Beckett had been there earlier and helped them get one going.

Whatever the case, Sterling finished the distance in record time. As he stood in front of the door, he thudded it loudly with one gloved hand while he unlatched his skis with the other. "Violet, open up. We need to talk."

He heard voices inside as he tossed aside his first ski. He finished with his second ski as Beckett came into view on the opposite side of the creek.

Sterling knocked against the door again. "Please, Violet. Whatever is wrong, we can work it out, can't we?"

The door cracked open, and Hyacinth's face appeared in the crack. "Hi, Sterling. It's about time."

It's about time? What did that mean?

Hyacinth peered beyond him, her gaze latching onto Beckett. Something flashed in her eyes. Was it interest? Or loathing? Sterling could never tell with those two.

"What's wrong?" Sterling asked. "Is Violet okay?"

"She will be in just a moment." Hyacinth moved back and then opened the door wider.

Sterling hesitated. "Is there any way I could talk

privately with her for a few minutes?"

Hyacinth motioned at him. "Just come in."

A tremor pulsed through him. He didn't want to be afraid, didn't want to be a coward, didn't want the bitterness and frustration to return and fill him. He needed to be stronger this time, needed to move forward with his resolve to love her unconditionally.

He took a deep breath and stepped inside.

Violet stood in the center of the cabin in the same green gown she'd worn a few days ago, her hair styled up. Her cheeks were flushed and her eyes shimmering…with fear but also something else.

The anxiety pounding inside Sterling grew suddenly quiet.

In a sweeping glance, he took in the cabin, still decorated with all the pretty things Violet and Hyacinth had made the last time they were here. But this time there were candles on the table, along with two place settings and a covered platter.

It was the same setup that he'd dreamed of when he'd been a young man and planning his proposal with his best friend Maverick Oakley. It was the same setup that Mav had arranged that day Sterling had brought Violet out and proposed to her.

What was Violet doing?

At a movement from behind him, Sterling shifted to find Reverend Livingston standing by the stove, rubbing his hands together. The strange horse belonged to the reverend. That's where Sterling had seen it.

But why was the reverend at the cabin?

Sterling turned back to Violet to find her on her knees, her gown pooling around her. "Sterling," she started, her voice quivering and her hand trembling as she held out a ring—a simple gold band.

His heartbeat stopped.

"I loved you almost from the moment we met." The words were nearly identical to what he'd spoken to her when he'd proposed that wintery day back in January.

A thrill whispered through him. Was she doing what he thought she was?

She nodded as though answering his unasked question. "I let my fears control me for too long. But I want you to know that I am choosing to move beyond all my fears, and I'm choosing you today and always…if you'll still have me."

A strange heat pricked the backs of his eyes. She was trying to move past all that had once controlled her, and he was proud of her for having the courage to do so.

She extended the ring further, this time without wavering. "I love you, Sterling. Will you marry me?"

The thrill was no longer just whispering inside him. It had escalated into a clamor that was pulsing through his whole body.

Behind him, Beckett stepped into the cabin and

closed the door. Everything began to make sense. Violet had planned this whole event, had arranged to come out to the cabin, and had wrangled Beckett into helping.

"Marry me, today," Violet said again, holding his gaze and letting him see the sincerity in hers. "Today. Here. Now."

Holy sweet heaven. Was this really happening? Or was he only dreaming?

With his pulse racing, his feet carried him across the room to her. As he reached her, he lowered himself to his knees, then captured her outstretched hand. Without breaking her gaze, he brought her hand to his lips and pressed a kiss into her palm.

Then he took the ring and slid it on his finger. "Yes, I'll marry you. Today. Here. Now."

She smiled, her shoulders sagging just a little, her relief easing the worry in her face.

"But only if you're sure." His heart welled with all the love that he'd tried to keep at bay, so full that his chest hurt with the pressure of it.

"I'm sure, Sterling." Her smile inched higher. "I've learned that love isn't always perfect. But I want to spend my life learning to love you better."

He stared for a long moment at his hand and the gold band that signified her willingness to love him. He'd never dreamed this would be possible with her. But what if everything had happened for a reason? What if their failed engagement and wedding had actually been a blessing that had pushed them both to mature in their love for each other?

He gently cupped her cheek. "I vow to learn to love you better too. With every passing day and year, I will love you until my dying breath."

Her eyes were wide and filled with something he'd wanted to see there but never had. Love.

He bent in and touched his lips to hers, pledging himself to her forever.

She was actually getting married. She was really doing it this time.

Violet stood beside Sterling at the center of the cabin, in front of Reverend Livingston. Compared to the burly cowboys in the room, the reverend seemed so small of stature. But he was kind and had been the first time she'd met him. Thankfully, he'd been willing to go along with her scheme and had accompanied Beckett on the ride from town to the cabin.

Next to her, Hyacinth acted as a witness, and Beckett was beside Sterling as a second witness. Beckett wasn't wearing his usual scowl, but he didn't seem happy about the union.

Violet didn't blame him for still having doubts about her intentions. Maybe it would take time to prove to him that she was a changed woman. Maybe it would take time to prove to herself that she was changing. She would likely still battle her fears at times. Like now…

She'd clasped her hands together to keep them from shaking, but beneath her voluminous skirt, her legs wobbled. Even so, she tried to focus on what the reverend was saying.

"Wilt thou have this man to be thy wedded husband," he said, "to live together after God's ordinance in the holy estate of Matrimony? Wilt thou obey him and serve him, love, honor, and keep him, in sickness and in health? And forsaking all others, keep thee only to him, so long as you both shall live?"

The anxiety in her chest was swirling and rising and starting to choke off the air in her lungs. She tried to draw in a breath, but she felt suddenly like she was drowning.

Sterling had already spoken his vows with certainty and strength. Why couldn't she do the same?

She closed her eyes and forced herself to remember all the qualities about Sterling she loved, all the many things that were so different from her father. Sterling was reliable and had roots and didn't run away from commitment. He loved her more than himself.

In the next instant, his arm gently circled behind her back, holding her up and being there for her in this moment of her past creeping back out to torment her.

Sterling was not her father. His presence was stable and his love steadfast. She couldn't forget that.

"Violet?" the reverend prompted gently.

She nodded, opened her eyes, then shifted so that she could see Sterling. "I will. I will. I will."

"Wonderful," said the reverend, his voice laced with relief.

Sterling's furrowed brow smoothed out a little, and he offered her a reassuring smile. His face was covered with thick, dark stubble, and his hair was mussed from his ride up to the cabin, but he'd never looked more appealing than at that moment.

"Now for the giving of the ring." The reverend held out his prayer book expectantly.

Sterling stared at it. Of course, he hadn't known he was getting married today, so why would he have brought a ring along. "I don't—"

"Here." Beckett placed a delicate band onto the book.

Sterling glanced at it, then nodded his thanks at Beckett.

Violet's breath snagged at the sight of it—a golden ring engraved with tiny, detailed flowers—violets. "It's beautiful." And thoughtful and perfect, just like him.

"I hope you don't mind," he said, "but it's the ring I had made for you previously."

"I love it. And I wouldn't want any other ring." It would stand as a reminder of all they'd gone through and all the ways they'd grown together.

The reverend cleared his throat. "Shall we continue?"

"Yes," she said at the same time as Sterling.

He smiled again, his warm brown eyes melting her. By the time he slid the ring down her finger, she was nothing more than a puddle on the floor.

Reverend Livingston led them through the rest of the ceremony, but it was a blur to Violet because all she could think about was how good Sterling was to her and how she wanted to prove herself worthy of his love.

After the reverend gave the benediction and final prayer, he closed his prayer book. "I now pronounce that you are man and wife, in the name of the Father, and of the Son, and of the Holy Ghost. Amen."

Sterling was watching her closely, as if gauging whether she might get spooked and run away. Beckett, too, had narrowed his eyes on her, and Hyacinth was holding Violet's arm, her grip tightening.

She was done running away from her problems. She knew of only one way to prove it to everyone. She lifted on her toes, wrapped her arms around Sterling's neck, and dragged him down into a kiss.

She fused her mouth with his, hoping to communicate to him that she was his wife now and that nothing would ever change that. She would never leave him and would always be by his side.

His mouth met hers eagerly, as though he understood the message she was trying to communicate and was giving her a message of his own: that he would always cherish her in a way that no man ever had before.

She could taste his power and hunger, and it stirred something within her, the desire for more. She pressed in closer, and his hands slid up her back.

"Save it for later," came Beckett's testy growl.

She broke away from Sterling first, the heat of embarrassment rushing through her at Beckett's bold insinuation. With a flush infusing her cheeks, she took a step away from Sterling.

He didn't let go of her, only shifting his hands to her waist. And he didn't take his eyes from her, the brown now hazy and hot, reaching across the distance to sear her.

"Time for us to go." Hyacinth gave Violet a half hug.

Violet was grateful Hyacinth had assisted her with all the wedding planning that morning, ensuring that everything had worked out just the way it should. She'd even asked Beckett to help them pull off the surprise, and he'd grudgingly agreed.

"Take all the time you need, boss." Beckett slapped Sterling good-naturedly on his back. "We brought up enough food to last you a week."

"A week?" Sterling's brow rose.

"For your honeymoon here at the cabin."

Sterling, for the first time, seemed to take in the supplies that they'd brought with them—food staples, clothing, fresh blankets, and more. He turned to his foreman and shook his hand.

After more hugs and thanks, Hyacinth, Beckett, and the reverend started out across the snow on their skis. Violet snuggled against Sterling's side as they stood in the doorway and watched them disappear through the snowy woodland.

When they were finally alone, Sterling bent down and pressed a kiss to her forehead. "I love you, wife."

She was his wife. A place inside her trembled—this time not in fear but in anticipation. "Are you hungry? I had Alonzo prepare your favorite meal."

Sterling wrapped both arms around her, pulled her inside, and then closed the door. "I'm very hungry. For you." He lowered his lips to hers and gave her a quick but voracious kiss.

Her chest ached with a hunger of her own. She wanted more of his kisses, more of him.

Taking in the table setting and special meal, he started to pull away.

She didn't let him go and instead smiled up at him. "There's only one thing I'd like right now."

He halted. "What's that?"

"More of your kisses."

A slow smile curved up his lips and filled his eyes. "I think I can oblige you."

"I hope so."

He tugged her back into his arms, lowered his mouth to hers, and obliged her to the fullest.

Author's Note

Dear Reader,

Big happy sigh. Isn't it a relief to finally see Sterling Noble and Violet Berkley get their long-overdue happily ever after? They both had a lot to work through in order to get to that point, but the journey made them both better and stronger as a result. I hope you enjoyed going on the journey with them.

You might be wondering who gets the next story? Of course Beckett deserves to find true love. So does Hyacinth. And they both will eventually, but you'll have to wait to find out if that's with each other!

The next book in the Noble Ranch series actually gives lonely veterinarian Thatcher Hoyt his love story, with a mail-order-bride mix-up that you won't want to miss. It's a sweet romance that brings two unlikely people together just in time for Christmas.

If you missed out on reading about Sterling and Violet's disastrous first wedding in *Waiting for the*

Rancher, then you're in luck! I've included the first chapter so that you can go back in time and get a glimpse of how their story started! While you're reading about the runaway bride and jilted groom, you'll get to meet Maverick Oakley, Sterling's childhood best friend. You might even like him enough to read about his falling in love with Hazel Noble (Sterling's little sister).

As always, I love hearing from YOU! If you haven't yet joined my Facebook Reader Room, what are you waiting for!? It's a great place to keep up to date on all my book releases and book news, as well as a fun place to connect with other readers and me.

Farewell, but not for long!

Make sure you didn't miss out on my High Country Ranch series. The books can be read as standalones, but they're even better read in order.

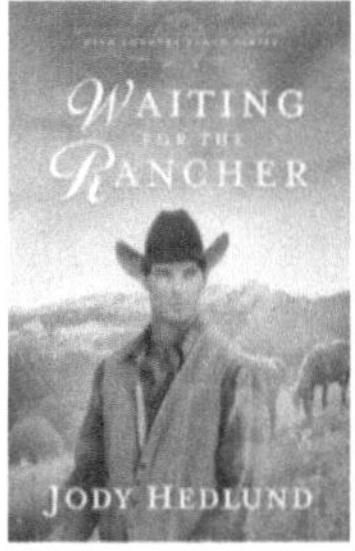

Waiting for the Rancher

Hazel Noble loves her job managing the mares at High Country Ranch. As the foaling season begins, she gets to spend even more time with the horses…and with her secret crush, Maverick Oakley, the owner of High Country Ranch and her brother Sterling's best friend. When Maverick unwittingly ruins Sterling's wedding, he goes from best friend to worst enemy. With the rift between their families, Maverick is faced with the possibility of losing Hazel, and he can no longer deny how much he's always cared about her.

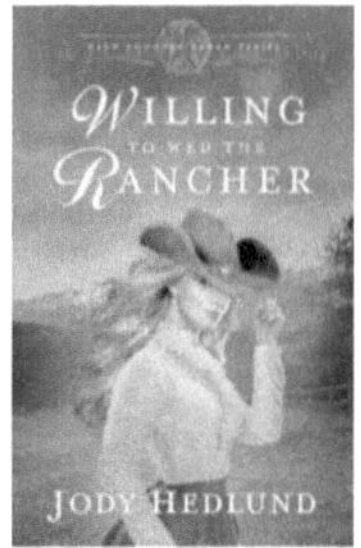

Willing to Wed the Rancher

Assistant schoolteacher Clarabelle Oakley has a hard time saying no. When Eric Meyer, widowed father of two of her young students, proposes to her, she botches her effort to tell him no and that she wants to marry for love, not convenience. Only days later, the unthinkable happens, and Clarabelle learns she's been given charge of Eric's children and his farm. Professor Franz Meyer arrives in Summit County, Colorado, to make peace with his estranged brother but discovers Eric is gone, leaving too many unanswered questions.

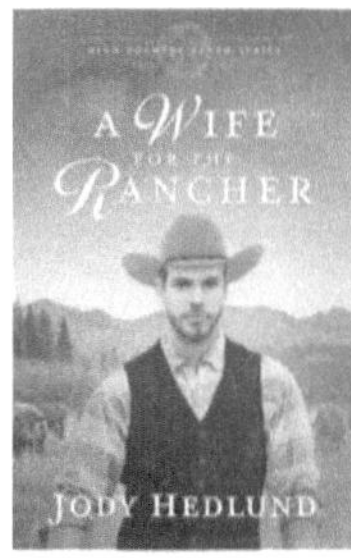

A Wife for the Rancher

Millionaire heiress, Genevieve Hollis, has everything she wants except one thing, freedom, because her guardian stepmother insists on overseeing every move she makes. When Genevieve sees a newspaper advertisement from a rancher seeking a mother for his baby, she jumps at the chance to escape. Ryder Oakley has suffered the repeated misfortune of losing the people he loves most, so now that he's a single father with a newborn baby, he's determined not to lose his son.

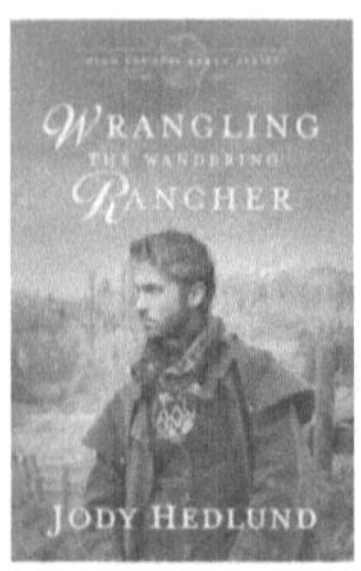

Wrangling the Wandering Rancher

Maisy Merritt has vowed she'll never marry a mountain man. Even though she loves the Colorado Rockies and the wild creatures she helps, she hates the way her pa's mountain-man ways take him away from his family. Maisy's ready to start a normal life, and that includes marrying a normal man. As a trapper and trail guide, Tanner Oakley lives a wandering life. He's decided that he's not husband material for any woman since he's so restless and unsettled.

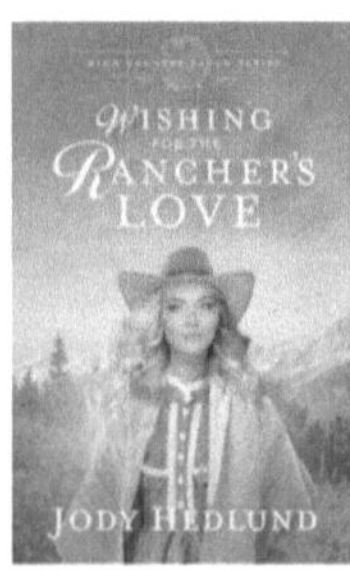

Wishing for the Rancher's Love

As the only one of her siblings who hasn't married, Clementine Oakley feels left behind. But she does her best to focus on her candy-making business in Worth's General Store. Giving and outgoing, she makes friends with everyone—except one person, the store owner's son…Grady Worth. Grady isn't sure why he can't get along with Clementine, but every time they're together, all they do is bicker. When his dad proposes a contest to encourage Grady to find love, Clementine is the last person he considers as an option.

READ ON FOR AN EXCERPT OF WAITING FOR THE RANCHER!!

Waiting
FOR THE
Rancher

JODY HEDLUND

HIGH COUNTRY RANCH SERIES

WAITING FOR THE RANCHER

JODY HEDLUND

NORTHERN LIGHTS PRESS

"Can't believe she's really gonna marry a scallywag like you." Maverick Oakley punched his best friend's arm. "She must be desperate."

Sterling Noble straightened his black string bow tie. "What can I say? I'm irresistible."

Maverick stuck a finger into his own bow tie and loosened it. Even then it still felt like it was strangling him, just like it had since the moment he'd put it on.

They stood side by side in front of the bureau mirror in the room Sterling had always shared with his brothers. Maverick was an inch or so shorter than his friend's six feet three inches, and he had leaner facial features with a square jawline and more prominent chin. His hair was darker—almost black—compared to Sterling's lighter brown, and he had blue eyes while Sterling's were brown.

Other than that, they both had rugged, muscular frames that came from years of hard work on their families' bordering ranches. Their skin was weathered from the sun and wind of Colorado's high country. Although most of the time they had a layer of scruff on their jaws, today, on Sterling's wedding day, they were both clean shaven.

Sterling was staring at himself, his eyes wide and filled with trepidation.

Maverick gave his friend a nod. "Violet's real lucky. You're a good man, the best. She couldn't ask for anyone better."

Beneath his collar and tie, Sterling's Adam's apple rose then fell. "Hope I can make her happy the way she deserves."

"You will."

A light rap sounded on the door.

Sterling didn't move, continued to examine himself as if he were counting his flaws and all the ways he didn't measure up.

"Come in." Maverick took charge for his friend, guessing he'd be nervous on his wedding day too. Not that he was getting married anytime soon. He hadn't cared about women, not for months. Not since his pa had died. He actually hadn't cared a whole heap about anything. Even today, he was having a hard time mustering the appropriate enthusiasm.

The door opened, and Hazel stepped into the room. "You fellows ready?"

Sterling's kid sister had her hair done up in a fancy style, with what appeared to be little pearls woven throughout. She was wearing a silvery gown that shimmered in the spring sunshine that was pouring through the room's tall window.

Maverick wasn't used to seeing her all gussied up. Most days at work, she wore her sturdy corduroy skirts, tall leather boots, a duster coat over a simple blouse, and a hat with her hair tucked up out of sight.

Even though he'd seen her nearly every day since she'd taken the position of broodmare manager last autumn, he rarely got a view of her fair hair, blond like a light-colored sorrel.

With her forehead puckered, her bronze-colored eyes swung between him and Sterling. "What's wrong?"

"Nothin'." He answered for Sterling, clamping his friend on his shoulder and squeezing. "We were about to head downstairs."

Hazel didn't respond, the sure sign she didn't believe him. That was the thing about Hazel—she could read emotions in people and animals better than anyone. It's what made her so good with horses and why his pa had hired her.

Maverick stuck a finger into his collar again, that

familiar strangling sensation returning. His pa wouldn't be at the wedding today because of him and his foolishness. His pa wouldn't be at any event ever again, big or little, important or not.

An ache swelled in Maverick's chest, and he drew in a quick breath to try to push it back down.

At his intake, Hazel's gaze softened. He hadn't told her what he was feeling, hadn't shared about the remorse that was turning into self-loathing, but he suspected she knew, almost as though she could visibly see his pain and understood why the day was hard for him.

Giving himself a hard mental shake, he grasped Sterling by the shoulder and began to guide him toward the door. "Let's go, big fella. Time to get hitched."

Sterling went along willingly. "Reckon you're right."

Hazel moved into the hallway and waved them ahead of her. Sterling took a step, but then paused in front of the door across the hall, where Violet was getting ready with her sister and mother.

She was perfect for Sterling in every way. He'd been crazy about her since the day her family had moved to Breckenridge and he'd first laid eyes on her a year ago.

The trouble was that Violet didn't adore Sterling to the same extent—at least, from what Maverick could tell. She was a real nice gal and all, but there were times when Maverick wasn't sure she was ready to settle down.

He'd been surprised when Sterling had proposed

marriage to her a few months ago, especially since the two hadn't been courting all that long. But Maverick had supported Sterling the way any best friend would. In fact, he'd even helped Sterling with his proposal plans, the plans they'd made when they'd been younger and had dreamed up how they'd each propose to the woman they fell in love with.

Sterling had decided he would propose by taking his true love skiing to nearby Devil's Glen, have a romantic dinner in an old miner's cabin there, and then ask her to marry him during dessert.

Maverick had been the one to ski out to the cabin ahead of time. He'd set up everything, including table linens, candles, and pine boughs to freshen the scent. He'd even brought the meal the Nobles' family cook had made. Maverick had ensured that every detail was perfect.

The January day had been beautiful, and the conditions had been just right. Sterling had proposed to Violet the way he'd always planned. The problem was Sterling had taken Violet by surprise, and she'd turned him down. He'd come back from the monumental event crushed.

The next weekend, Violet had apologized to him and accepted the proposal. Course, Sterling loved her enough to put aside his disappointment and had given her the ring again.

Now with the coming of April, the big day had arrived.

Sterling hesitated in the hallway. Was he thinking of stopping and talking with Violet?

Maverick steered him away from the door. "Naw, you don't get to see her yet."

Sterling shuffled forward. "Just wanted to talk to her through the door and make sure she's all right."

"Everything's fine." Maverick gave him a shove. "Now c'mon."

Sterling nodded, as though trying to convince himself that everything really was fine. Then he started down the stairs, and Maverick trailed him with Hazel on his heels.

Family and friends were milling about in the entryway of the Nobles' sprawling ranch house. The double doors leading to the front parlor were open, revealing more guests waiting for the start of the ceremony.

In years past, Maverick's whole family would have been at a gathering like this. His pa and ma and five siblings. But today…

His gaze snagged on his twin sisters, Clementine and Clarabelle, who were seated on a settee just inside the parlor where they were chatting with Mrs. Noble. Besides himself, they were the only Oakleys at the wedding. And Clarabelle had almost stayed home because she hadn't wanted to leave Ma's bedside.

Ma's pale face and listless body flashed to the front of his mind. Not only had his foolishness cost Pa his life, but it was costing Ma hers too. She was dying of a broken heart, and with each passing day, she was only getting worse.

Sterling finished descending amidst warm congratulations, but Maverick paused near the bottom of the stairway and swallowed hard.

What was more, without Pa there, the family was falling apart, and it was all because of him.

Maybe he hadn't been directly responsible for all that had happened to cause the big rift between Ryder and Tanner, but if Pa had been there, he would have known what to do to make them see reason. In fact, his two younger brothers probably wouldn't have started fighting at all, not with Pa intervening and bringing about peace.

At a gentle hand on his shoulder, Maverick shifted to find Hazel on the step above him. Her warm gaze seemed to encourage him that everything would be all right.

But he knew the truth deep inside. Nothing would ever be all right again.

He pulled at his tie, loosening it another notch. Even then, his breathing turned shallow, and he couldn't seem to get enough air.

With franticness rising inside, he glanced around for an escape and locked in on the front door. He needed to step outside…for a few seconds.

He broke away from Hazel's hold and descended the last couple of steps. "Be right back." He tossed her what he hoped was a grateful look. "Need a fresh lungful."

She was peering at her mother, who was motioning at her to hurry. "Don't take too long. Everyone is waiting for the wedding to start."

He was already winding his way past the guests to the front door. Although he was tempted to remind Hazel he wasn't holding things up, that Violet and Sterling were the ones dallying, he bit back his comment and pushed out the door.

He stepped onto the wraparound porch that faced Bald Mountain and the range lining the eastern part of Summit County. The rocky peaks were covered in a thick layer of snow that the high-altitude sun was slowly beginning to melt away.

The pasture spreading out in front of the Nobles' house was still barren and brown with patches of snow piled in the shade of boulders or brush. Hints of green were beginning to make an appearance, but it would be another month before blue grama grass began to flourish again.

As he crossed the porch and started down the steps, he sucked in a deep breath of the cool air. The dampness of soil and the waft of cattle and manure filled his nostrils.

He wasn't ready for the wedding, wasn't ready to be around everyone, wasn't ready for going on with life as if everything was the same as it had always been when it had all changed.

He followed the flagstone path forward several feet.

Then he halted and inhaled again, his sights on the towering range ahead. If only he could be as strong and solid as the mountains, just like his pa. But he was all too often hotheaded and hasty.

Squaring his shoulders, he stuffed his hands into his trouser pockets. As he swept his gaze over the beauty of the wild mountain valley, the sadness in his chest spread into his limbs. Although he loved the high country, no one had loved it more than Pa.

For the past fourteen years since leaving their horse farm in Kentucky, Pa had done everything he could to build a new life for his family in Colorado. After years of hard work, Pa had finally begun to see the rewards of his efforts. The High Country Ranch—or High C Ranch, as it was called—had gained a reputation for having the best horses in the state, possibly even in the West.

Maverick gave a shake of his head, as if that could somehow shake away the melancholy. He couldn't make today about him and his sorrow and regrets. This was Sterling's special day, and he had to be there for his friend and not stand outside feeling sorry for himself.

He shifted to return inside, but at the sight of a woman in a cream-colored gown leaning against the side of the house, he paused. The dark hair and pale skin were all he needed to recognize Violet.

What was she doing outside?

She had a handkerchief out and was blotting the

corners of her eyes, almost as if she were crying. What was wrong? Was she having pre-wedding jitters?

An urgency prodded him. He couldn't let Sterling see his bride like this, outside, crying. It would only make him more nervous.

Maverick shot a glance toward the front door, then to the parlor window. He could take care of this without Sterling being any the wiser. He'd talk to Violet and encourage her to go in right away and proceed with the wedding.

He veered off the path and strode across the flat tufts of grass. The dampness muted his bootsteps so that he was almost upon Violet before she glimpsed him nearing.

She pushed away from the house and rapidly began to dry her cheeks. "Hi, Maverick."

He stopped a foot away from her.

She averted her face and continued to blot at her eyes. "What are you doing out here?"

With his hands still stuffed into his pockets, he gave a slight shrug. He couldn't very well admit that he'd been overcome with guilt over his pa and family. She didn't need to hear that today. "Came lookin' for you, darlin'." The words were out before he could stop them. "Wanted to make sure you're okay."

She lifted her eyes, which gave him full view of the angst clouding them. "I don't know what I'm doing."

"I do. You're gonna go in there and marry the man you love."

"But how do I know if I really love him?"

How could she not love Sterling? The fellow was one of the kindest and most giving men Maverick had ever known. "Listen—"

"What if I have feelings for someone else too?" She straightened and seemed to pull in a steadying breath.

"You're just nervous. That's all."

"No. It's not all." She blinked back more tears. "I haven't been as sure about Sterling as he's been about me."

Maverick's gut cinched. He was glad Sterling wasn't nearby to hear the confession. "Don't matter none. Sterling's got enough love for the both of you." That was the plain truth. Sterling had been a goner since the day he'd laid eyes on Violet.

"I don't want to hurt Sterling." She pressed a hand against the long row of covered buttons that ran up the front of her bodice until she reached the brooch at the neckline. "But I just don't think I'm ready for this."

This conversation wasn't going the way Maverick wanted, and he had to do something—anything—to assure Violet that Sterling was the right man for her. He scrambled to find a solution. Maybe he oughta pick her up and carry her inside.

Without giving himself—or her—a chance to protest, he bent and swept her up into his arms. "C'mon. I'm taking you back in."

As he situated her against his chest, she wrapped her arms around his neck. Her skirt was full and the layers of material cumbersome, forcing him to hold her closer to keep from dropping her. He rounded the house and headed back toward the front door.

Her arms tightened with each step, and she lifted her head so that her cheek brushed against his. "Please. We need to talk."

At the plea in her voice, he halted. He dropped his gaze to find that she was looking up at him with furrowed brows. She was such a pretty woman. Not that he was attracted to her, but that didn't mean he couldn't admit she had stunning features, with pale skin that made her eyes and hair all the more vibrant.

"You're a good man," she whispered.

"Course I am." He offered her what he hoped was an encouraging smile.

She studied his face, ending up at his mouth. "You have such a nice smile."

"So do you, darlin'." He let his smile widen, hoping he could cheer her up. "I'd sure love to see your pretty lips smile right about now."

Her eyes only welled with more tears. "Oh, Maverick."

"I said I wanna see your smile, not tears." He gentled his voice.

"I think I have feelings for you too." Her arms

tightened around his shoulders.

"Whoa, now." What was going on here?

Her gaze trailed his face again. "I've tried to ignore the feelings, but they just won't go away."

"Don't go saying things like that." He lowered his voice to a hiss. This was bad. Real bad. Worse than bad.

"You can't deny you've been feeling things for me too." Her fingers at the back of his neck crept into his hair.

He had to fix things quick-like, before the situation went downhill even more. "Now darlin'—"

She rose up and pressed her lips to his, cutting him off. Her mouth was soft and her kiss filled with desperation. Her hands in his hair dragged him down, and at the same time, she deepened her kiss.

Maverick couldn't move. The shock of the moment paralyzed him. What was Violet doing? Why was she kissing him? And how could he help her see the error of her way? Help her realize the only man she oughta be kissing was Sterling?

At the banging of the front door and Sterling's shout, Maverick's heart plummeted. No doubt his friend was witnessing this whole interaction with Violet.

Maverick's muscles stiffened. He couldn't let Sterling find out the truth, that Violet had been the one to initiate the kiss. It would break his heart.

There was only one way to keep Sterling from

suspecting Violet had cheated on him. Maverick pressed into her. He'd take the blame for the kiss, act like it was his idea.

The instant he let his lips fuse with hers, he knew the plan was foolish, that it wouldn't work. That he couldn't kiss her in return, not for any reason. But before he could pull back, Sterling was grabbing his arm and wrenching Violet from him.

**GRAB YOUR COPY OF THE NOVEL TO
READ MORE!**

Jody Hedlund is the bestselling author of more than sixty novels and is the winner of numerous awards. Jody lives in Michigan with her husband, busy family, and five spoiled cats. She writes sweet historical romances with plenty of sizzle.

A complete list of my novels can be found at jody hedlund.com.

Would you like to know when my next book is available? You can sign up for my newsletter, become my friend on Goodreads, like me on Facebook, or follow me on Instagram.

Newsletter: jodyhedlund.com
Facebook: AuthorJodyHedlund
Instagram: @JodyHedlund